HIDDEN LIGHT

HIDDEN LIGHT

Earl Shurtz

iUniverse, Inc.
New York Lincoln Shanghai

Hidden Light

iUniverse books may be ordered through booksellers or by contacting:

iUniverse
2021 Pine Lake Road, Suite 100
Lincoln, NE 68512
www.iuniverse.com
1-800-Authors (1-800-288-4677)

ISBN-13: 978-0-595-36767-2
ISBN-10: 0-595-36767-4

Printed in the United States of America

CONTENTS

▼

Chapter 1: Washington D.C., April 2005, David & Nancy 1

Chapter 2: New York City, David & Dr. Warren 5

Chapter 3: Washington D.C., Nancy Reilly, Monsignor Averti 8

Chapter 4: Opus Dei 11

Chapter 5: Bavaria—2001, Dr. Heinlin 14

Chapter 6: The Village at The Abby of Etal: David meets Maria,
2001 17

Chapter 7: The Castle, 2001 Lotar Herron 22

Chapter 8: The Vatican Information, 2005 Nancy Reilly,
Monsignor Averti 24

Chapter 9: Opus Dei Headquarters, New York 2005 Guido 27

Chapter 10: The Medieval Castle 2001 David, Lotar 30

Chapter 11: Dominick Averti at age thirteen 1968 32

Chapter 12: Washington, D.C., May 2005 David, Nancy 35

Chapter 13: The Castle, near The Abby of Etal, Bavaria 2001,
David, Maria 39

Chapter 14: David and Maria in Bavaria 2001, Angelina, Bishop
Rhein 45

Chapter 15: Washington D.C. May, 2005 Nancy, Ruth, David 51

Chapter 16:   David Schilling as a child circa 1960—year 2001
Bishop Rhein Revelation 54

Chapter 17:   The Alpine Village, Bavaria 2001, David, Maria 57

Chapter 18:   The Castle, Village, Abby of Etal 2001—David's
meeting with Otto Heinlin. Maria turned away. 59

Chapter 19:   Santa Fe, New Mexico 2005 Nancy's wilderness
experience 65

Chapter 20:   Castle Inn—2001 Murder 72

Chapter 21:   The Killer 77

Chapter 22:   David's release 2001 79

Chapter 23:   Dominick Averti—2005 Vatican
Archives—Flashback 81

Chapter 24:   Washington D.C., 2005—David and Nancy 86

Chapter 25:   Maria, Berlin 2005 90

Chapter 26:   New York 2005 Guido's Dilemma 93

Chapter 27:   David Schilling, His Other Side. Washington
D.C. 2005 96

Chapter 28:   David at home in Ohio 2005 103

Chapter 29:   Dominick Averti—Rome 1978 107

Chapter 30:   Nancy, Flight to Paris—Guido, 2005 111

Chapter 31:   Maria's search for information 113

Chapter 32:   Nancy in Paris, Departure for Rome 116

Chapter 33:   David's preparation, Trip to Europe, Adventure in
Rome 133

Chapter 34:   Maria at the Castle Inn—Bavaria 155

Chapter 35:   Opus Dei Headquarters, New York 159

Chapter 36:   Bishop Rhein and Maria 161

Chapter 37: Convergence on Rome, David, Gloria Peole, Nancy's arrival 166

Chapter 38: Rome—the next day 170

Chapter 39: The Pope and the Bishop 173

Chapter 40: In the Archives 175

Chapter 41: The Conflict 179

Chapter 42: The Meeting 183

Chapter 43: The Revelations 186

CHAPTER 1

▼

WASHINGTON D.C., APRIL 2005, DAVID & NANCY

David Schilling was not aware that he was being followed. At six foot two he was trimmed down to a muscular 215 pounds. Dressed in Khakis, with all the pockets, he looked like someone going on safari.

He crossed the electronic security system with the idea of intense research in the private specialty library.

"May I help you sir?"

He looked around for the location of the voice.

An attractive, tall, blond woman, in her forties, stepped from behind the shelves, where she was filing books in the Anthropology section.

David was startled, "Uh, I am looking for information on symbology."

"What period? Are you looking for something based on religion?" Her penetrating blue eyes displayed a serious note as she came closer.

"I am doing research for a book, a novel."

"Please follow me. Maybe I can help you to a specific section." She turned and started away while he was composing himself. Wow, she didn't look like any librarian he had seen. Of course, the world of library science was becoming highly technical, and with better salaries, bright and energetic people were lured to the profession.

He followed her down the aisle, noticing her trim, tight fitting skirt, and shapely legs. Trying to focus on the project, at hand, he saw a section of books that interested him. "Miss, could we stop here for a minute?"

She stopped, turned, and walked back to him. He was already pulling a book from the shelf. She came close enough for him to catch the aroma of her perfume, and from the corner of his eye, noticed the well developed bust, defined by a white blouse, all accented by her navy blue uniform.

David Schilling, in his early sixties, had spent years visiting libraries, churches, synagogues, pyramids, museums, art galleries, government centers, and other concentrations of data concerning religion, the life of Christ, and socio-government factors affecting the lives of today's world population.

Divorced eight years ago, he began his world research tour in earnest. When he sold his real estate holdings there was enough after taxes for him to live comfortably. With no wife, and his children grown, he was able to travel about freely.

"Did you find something?"

He cleared his throat to avoid the squeak in his voice, common when he encountered, and was first near, an attractive woman. "I think I should look around this section to get some better ideas, so I don't waste your time."

She moved even closer to peer over his shoulder at the book he held. His natural shyness, at times inconvenient to him, seemed to attract women. He seldom made a first or aggressive move with them. "That is what I am here for. I would be happy to help." She stepped back.

He asked, "Is there a table where I could review some of these books?"

"Sure, she said, just pull the ones forward that you are interested in, I'll help you carry them and lead you to a private area."

There was really no reason for David to be shy. He was educated, tall, with thin graying hair, turquoise eyes, financially secure, and above average looking. An avid outdoorsman, he had been a pilot for thirty years, played tennis, rode motorcycles, loved hiking, and went scuba diving on a regular basis. Yet, in psychological counseling his therapist was puzzled by this shyness trait, indicated from the results of his written personality test.

After two hours of pouring intently through a stack of books, he looked up and Miss Reilly was standing at his table, smiling. "Are there any of these books you would like to check out? We are closing in ten minutes."

He looked quickly at his watch, not believing it was almost ten o'clock P.M. He smiled rather seriously and said, "No, I have been taking notes and have to leave the hotel early in the morning to fly to New York. I wouldn't be able to return the books on time. By the way, where do I call a taxi to the Clarion Hotel?"

"Taxis are really slow at this location, particularly when it's raining, like tonight. I am going right by there on my way home. Could I drop you off?"

"Oh no; I don't want to put you to that trouble."

"It's no trouble at all. We can chat about your research project. You see, that subject was my major and a special interest."

By the time they arrived at the hotel he had found out that Nancy Reilly was forty-nine years old, had masters degrees in both history and library science and was planning a doctorate program in the history of religion. She was divorced, with a grown daughter, Ruth, at the University, and liked jogging, horses and the outdoors.

During the ride he revealed that he was pursuing startling revelations about the life of Christ, Mary Magdalene and the Bible. He wasn't quite sure how far to go with this subject for he often received strange responses from friends, strangers, and colleagues.

Nancy became rather quiet when he mentioned this, but smiled cheerfully and gave him her card, after stopping at the hotel entrance. "I have some thoughts and some of my own research on your subject. If you have time, call me when you return to Washington."

Surprised, he thanked her profusely, and said he would call her. Neither of them noticed the car following. It stopped and pulled over to the curb about a half block away, lost in the rain and the headlights of other traffic.

Nancy drove to her apartment building. As she turned into the underground garage, the car following noted the location, and then sped by.

CHAPTER 2

▼

NEW YORK CITY, DAVID & DR. WARREN

David slept well except for a phone call in the middle of the night. There was no response when he answered so he hung up assuming it was a wrong number. He dressed in another khaki outfit with epaulettes on the shirt and lots of pockets. He didn't care about the glances when he wore these clothes because they were practical to wash and dry with the new micro fiber fabrics. The pockets were convenient for passports, tickets and notes.

He usually stayed at the Algonquin Hotel on Forty-Fourth Street, because of its central location. The cats lounging in the lobby ignored him as he finished his morning newspaper in one of the comfortable stuffed chairs. The history of the writers and actors that congregated here over the years added to the ambiance and the homey atmosphere in the lobby and restaurant area. He took his last sip of coffee, brushed off the crumbs of his pastry, started for the elevator, and accidentally bumped into a man who had been watching him.

In the cab ride to Columbia University he thought back over his years of research, particularly the most recent ones. His idea to publish a novel was bold and controversial. He couldn't share much of his information with religious scholars because their cooperation stopped when they suspected his subject. Consequently he had to use subterfuge when dealing with major libraries. The archives at Columbia had critical information in its anthropology and archaeology departments.

Dr. Trent Warren, head of the anthropology department, had been David's army buddy, resulting in a life long friendship. He could provide access to manuscripts that were not available for public use. Many of these were questionable in the accuracy of their content and the validity of their origin. The ones that were known to the Columbia faculty were in danger of being banished from the University campus.

Trent was a genius from a normal mid western family. He was tall, thin, and rather stooped. His life was books, research, teaching and writing. The books he had published were popular with academia and in the classroom.

As David walked through the campus and into Dr. Warren's office foyer he was surprised at the lack of security and administrative protocol. He knocked on the glass pane of Trent's office door and was greeted with a shout, "Come in." His desk was a jumble of papers.

"My God, Trent, you are up to your ass in papers as usual."

"David, come in quickly and lock the door. I have something urgent to tell you." Trent looked worried and gestured, *sit down.*

"What's wrong? You look like you have seen a ghost." David sat his briefcase down on the floor.

"David, I don't know if I can help you with your project."

"What? Why not?"

Trent leaned over the desk closer to David and lowered his voice. "I have received some strange phone calls saying things like, *David Schilling is in danger and so will you be if you give him information.* They always hang up when I try to talk"

David just looked at him, puzzled.

"Then I found this note in my office desk drawer, *persist with the books and tragedy will befall you and yours.*"

"What do they mean?" asked David although he already suspected.

Trent paused and said, "Otto, with all his idiosyncrasies, while gathering the lost and unpublished books written for the Bible, made lots of enemies. You were with him shortly before he died, suddenly, after the rumors became circulated that he had these books. His threats to expose biblical scholars and the church for concealing the truth got him killed and placed you in jeopardy."

David countered, "We know he was cantankerous and very unorthodox. Who would have believed him?" Dr. Otto Heinlin was a controversial but brilliant professor, who came to Columbia after the anthropology department in his German university asked him to leave. Here, his friendship with Trent Warren and the collaboration on research projects developed.

"Apparently some very powerful members of the church are fearful of losing their historic power base." Dr. Warren's hands were shaking as he became more agitated.

"Marlene has also received these phone calls at home and is insisting that I either go on a year sabbatical or retire."

"Oh, Trent, you can't do that. Isn't there some other way?"

"Marlene is so frightened she is threatening to leave me."

David held up his hands in a "stop" motion, "Wait, wait, Trent. Let's slow down. Let me think about this overnight at the hotel and I will call you in the morning."

"Okay David but take care what you say on the phone. I am beginning to suspect it may be bugged."

CHAPTER 3

▼

WASHINGTON D.C.,
NANCY REILLY,
MONSIGNOR AVERTI

Nancy Reilly finished her thirty minute run, left her jogging group and ran across the street to her apartment. She didn't notice the man watching her while pretending to look in the lower level shop window. She checked her answering machine for a call from her daughter before taking a quick shower to be at work by nine o'clock A.M. She split her shifts at the library between day shifts and late afternoon and evening ones.

"Nancy, her former husband said over the machine, I need to talk with you. Both Ruthie and I have received strange phone calls about you. Call me; it's urgent!" *What the heck?* Frank was always dramatic and disapproving of her. *I don't have time now. I will call him later.*

It was a bright sunny day, with the Cherry Blossoms exploding in color. Washington D.C., at times, could be the most vibrant and beautiful city in the universe. Nancy left the subway station at the end of rush hour, walking briskly, with her briefcase and her huge purse. She had lots of projects on her mind at the library, including her own personal research work and her planning for the Doctorate program. Pre-occupied, she didn't notice the short, stocky man following her. He was dressed in dark clothing and a wide brimmed hat pulled down over his forehead, shading the swarthy features of his face and eyes.

She entered the library off K Street with the noises of early morning traffic behind her. The elevator to the second floor was slow in arriving. The elevator doors seemed to sense when she was in a hurry and go into an automatic slow-down mode. Customarily elevator occupants self consciously avoid eye contact and the acknowledgement of others presence, no matter how crowded; this morning was no exception.

She thought, *Henry David Thoreau must have had experience in elevators. The confinement magnifies the insecurities of persons on their way to jobs and appointments. They are pumped up, suited, starched, painted, and prepared for events when they would rather be barefoot in a field of clover. "The mass of men live lives of quiet desperation", could be tattooed in the hearts and on the foreheads of all them. If I smile, make a joke, and make eye contact when entering an elevator, the experience is either the ultimate in rejection or a puncture in the balloon of relief, when the tension is broken.*

Entering her private office, she placed her heavy purse and briefcase on the credenza behind her desk, and went immediately to the schedule on the palm desktop at her computer. The week was packed with appointments and deadlines. She had to plan a telephone call to the Vatican, in Rome, about one of her research projects and needed to know the time differences from Eastern Standard.

The message light was blinking on her phone but she decided to ignore it.

"Operator, I need to place a call to Rome, Italy, person to person, to Monsignor Averti, at the Vatican." I am not sure of the time difference but it needs to be before closing hours, there, say, before four o'clock in the afternoon." Nancy had met Dominick Averti, a high ranking scholar at the Vatican archives, at a symposium while pursuing her Master's degree in Library Science.

"Yes Ma'am, it is, lets see, two-fifteen P.M. in London England, so it would be four-fifteen P.M. in Rome, I think. Please hold while I check the time zones."

Monsignor Averti had been at Harvard, in Boston, doing research work, for historic archive preservation. He and Nancy struck up a friendship while being seated next to each other at a small, select, group at a symposium round-table.

"Ma'am, it is four-fifteen in Rome. Do you want me to place the call now?"

Averti was handsome, with a very engaging personality. His smile and his graciousness were more like a movie star than a cleric. *How could this charming man devote his life to the church and to celibacy?* she thought.

After a series of answers, and call forwarding at the Vatican, the operator announced that the Monsignor was on the line.

"Hello, Nancy," the rich baritone voice said in slightly accented English. "How are you?"

"Monsignor, I am so glad I caught you, with the time differences I was unsure. I am fine. It is so nice to hear your voice." She had this strange flushing sensation that happened the first time she met him.

"And you, Nancy, how is your work going? How is your family?"

She didn't know much about his background but it seemed to be a non-traditional approach in the Catholic Church. His air of mystery, was accentuated by his good looks, and the brilliance of his works in ancient history.

She heard a faint clicking sound on the telephone but thought it was just the trans-Atlantic connection.

CHAPTER 4

▼

OPUS DEI

David's travel experiences and research over the years had caused him to develop information into theory.

Since its beginning, in Spain in 1928, the Opus Dei secret society, and its fanaticism, has been rumored. Catholic zealotry has been accused and denied in connection with the Inquisitions and the Crusades. The life and the death of Jesus Christ and his close relationships have been alleged to be extremely different from the popular beliefs of Christendom.

With the Catholic Church's effort to erase conflicting views over the centuries, Jose Maria Escriva de Balaquer, a Catholic priest, founded Opus Dei. It often operates outside the established order of the Church with secrecy and independence. Its role for women is in conflict with the intentions of Christ, as portrayed in the "lost books" of the Bible.

Opus Dei, with its extremist views, appeared to be the enforcement arm of the Catholic Church, in conflict with the Priory of Scion, founded in 1099 A.D. Some of the famous members of the Priory of Scion, included Sir Isaac Newton, Botticelli, Victor Hugo, and Leonardo Da Vinci. The mission of the Priory has been to renew the feminist equality, as intended by Christ and to keep the secret books and archives from being destroyed by the Church.

The Knights Templar, originally founded to be the enforcer for the Catholic Church, later changed roles, because of persecution by the Pope, to shed the light of truth to the teachings of Christ. To this day they have secret passwords conveyed only by mouth to ear in direct contact, developed for fear of being overheard and put to death. These secret orders were developed for protection from the militant forces of Catholicism.

David had joined the Masonic Lodge when he was twenty-one, and later was inducted to the Knights Templar order, but didn't understand the historic significance of the ritual and the real necessity of its origin.

Fear struck him as he awakened to an overcast morning. *Could there be significance to Trent's paranoia or am I just inferring too many unrelated coincidences together from my project?*

Shaking off the thoughts David took another sip of his coffee and stepped into the hot shower.

From DeVinci's painting of the "Last Supper" the images at the table were clear to him. Instead of twelve males, Mary Magdalene was on Jesus' right and was being physically threatened by one of the disciples. His research had caused him to believe that she was the designated person to carry forward the works and teachings of Christ. After Jesus' death she was maligned by some of the disciples in an effort to neutralize her power. The feminist presence displayed in symbology was diffused by accusations that she was a prostitute. The name in the legend at the bottom of the fresco was labeled "Giovanni" for the person in her position at the table. There are many accounts in history of the Epiphany and some confusion as to the names and the actual position of the disciples at the table.

Jesus' brother, James, one of his siblings, sired children to continue the bloodline of Jesus' family. The rumor that Jesus had had offspring was denied and expunged from many of the books edited to comprise the modern day Bible. King Constantine held such power that he actually assembled the Bible to his liking and tried to destroy the other books that had conflicting accounts of the history. Constantinople in Turkey, now Istanbul, was a city built on the ancient Greek site of Byzantium, by the Romans in 330 A.D., and structured by Constantine to be a major Christian center. The Greeks had previously occupied this country where Europe borders Asia. The city is actually in both continents, divided by the Bosporus Straits. The economic importance of great natural harbors and the status of being the only warm water sea port from the Black Sea have kept the Russians and forces of Christianity and the Moslems battling over the area for centuries.

Tales of the lost books had been rumored, and found in various places over the last two millenniums until now. They were discredited and vilified by the Church. Only sub-rosa organizations and archives had the books or parts of them.

CHAPTER 5

▼

BAVARIA—2001, DR. HEINLIN

"Dr. Heinlin I have had a very difficult time finding you." David and Otto Heinlin were sitting on a bench under a very large shade tree at the Abby of Etal in Bavaria.

"The Benedictines do not wish intrusion into their daily cloister." Otto Heinlin was portly, bearded, in his late fifties, and seemed pre-occupied.

"I understand sir." David shifted uneasily on the bench and waited.

Finally Dr. Heinlin asked, "What do you want with me?"

"Sir the subject is very delicate, I hope not to offend you, but I am told that you are a great authority on history of religions."

Otto just stared at David, not blinking.
"Should I go on?" David said, in a hesitant manner.

"Please get to your point. I have meditative sessions scheduled." His English was excellent with a combination of German and London based accents.

David cleared his throat, "You see I have been working on studies about the life of Christ, his family and the missing books of the Bible."

Otto jumped up from the bench and began to walk away.

"No, please, it is very important I talk with you."

"Who are you? How do I know you? Who sent you?"

"Sir, you don't know me. I am here on a strictly private matter and was very hopeful you would talk with me. Dr. Trent Warren from Columbia University in New York gave me your name."

"Hmm, Warren, I know him. How do I know he sent you?"

"I have this letter he sent with me for introduction." David pulled the letter from his briefcase and handed it to Dr. Heinlin.

Heinlin looked at the letter and said, "How do I know if this is his hand writing, and from him?"

"We can place a call from your phone to his office in New York."

"You could have anyone waiting at a New York telephone pretending to be Warren."

David hesitated, "Don't you have any issues or communications that only you and he know?"

Heinlin, was still standing apart from me, his penetrating blue eyes framed by his bushy eyebrows, narrowed, and he said in a very low voice, after a pause, "Yes, but nothing that can be said over the telephone."

"Dr. Heinlin, I am sure you don't remember this, but I met you in 1983 at Giza in Cairo. I was there with my former wife visiting pyramids, tombs, the Valley of the Kings and traveling the Nile River."

Heinlin's fixed stare indicated a light of recognition. He stood poised to leave.

"You were on the cruise boat on the Nile, when I had lost my wallet with all my cash, in the bar. I didn't discover my loss until the next morning. I went to the desk on the boat and reported it, and they said, *Oh yes, we have it.* Everything was intact." I was surprised at the honesty and when I asked, they told me that you had found the wallet and turned it in."

"You refused to accept a reward, but did let me buy you a drink at the bar. We had a long conversation about Egypt and my interest about the similarities at historic Mayan sites in the Yucatan Peninsula, with pyramids and astrology. It was your conversation that created an interest that has led me to writing a novel about the history of religion."

Heinlin relaxed slightly, and took a step towards me. "I will be leaving here next Friday. Can you meet me at the Inn in the Village that evening?"

We agreed upon the place and a time. This would give me a few days to continue my research. My curiosity was going to make it very difficult to wait.

Chapter 6

▼

The Village at The Abby of Etal: David meets Maria, 2001

Maria Albrecht was deep in thought, enjoying the warm sunny morning on the castle patio with her tea and pastries. She had arrived last night after a long car trip from Munich. Exhausted, she slept well in the big feather bed, through the deliciously cool night. Her theatre career was beginning to fulfill her dreams. At thirty-four, she had been married for a short time, divorced, and just unwinding from an affair. Her morning clothes were the latest in fabrics and designed for comfortable but colorful travel wear.

After a long hot shower she dried and combed out her medium length auburn hair, and sprayed on her new cologne. With a final look in the mirror she decided not to apply lipstick or make up. She was one of the fortunate few that looked fresh and attractive either way.

The words were still ringing in her ears, "Maria, your performance was seen by important theatre people. I can negotiate a contract for a starring role in a play that will run for twenty weeks in Berlin or I can get you a major movie part. Your career is about to take a giant leap."

She was at the crossroads of decision whether to continue in theatre or give up and face a business career. The visions of a home and family were still in her mind. She had a few days off before her next performance and needed time to think. Hans, her latest boy friend, was a body builder, with blond hair, younger, and very self centered. He was her trainer at the gymnasium. She was immediately attracted to his good looks and his charm. After a year long affair, he proved to be shallow and not some one she wanted a longer term relationship with.

The village, high on a slope, over looked beautiful green farm fields and a waterway that was carefully tended. Small boats carried tourists and farm produce. Locks were visible where the river intersected with the canal. The half timbered houses, characteristic of the area, created a storybook charm. The Castle at the edge of the town backed up to a deep forest.

On David's first day in the area, his thoughts were *how much the countryside resembled his native Ohio with the green fields and roadways.* As he drove up to the steps of the Castle he remembered how the guide book described the historic significance and gave it a good rating as an Inn and dining experience. The walkway was paved with cobble stones and led through an arbor to the entrance with heavy wood doors, strengthened by steel straps. The stained glass windows, with bars, were reflecting the sunlight that passed through the arbor. One door was open.

He passed through the doors into the hallway. There was a curving staircase directly ahead, a dining room and bar to the right, and a parlor to the left. No one was visible so he just stood there looking at a poster of an opera and the featured stars from Munich.

While waiting, he looked back out the entrance doors, to the bottom of the slope at the railway. There was a train stopping at a small station to pick up passengers. To his right, through the dining room windows, he could see an attractive young woman sitting in the sun on the patio with her morning tea. She was dressed differently from the Village persons he had seen—more colorful and fashionable.

He was about to take a few steps in her direction when he heard, "Good morning, welcome to the Castle." He was a big man with a warm smile and resembled one of the persons in the opera poster. "Are you looking for a room or lunch?" He obviously recognized me as an American, and spoke in heavily accented, but correct, English. He had appeared from a hallway under the stairs.

Out of habit, I spoke loudly and slowly thinking this was the way to be understood in a foreign country. "I am going to be here for a week and need room accommodations but I haven't eaten this morning. Is it possible to get breakfast or lunch?"

"Yes sir, would you like to be seated in the dining room or on the patio? After breakfast I can show you our rooms so you may choose one that you like?"

"That would be wonderful, the patio will be fine. Thank you."

"If you will find a seat, I will send a waitress. Then I will be back with the keys when you are finished."

I walked through the dining room to the patio and took a table, near, but not facing Maria.

She looked around, smiled and nodded. I simply said, "Good morning." My bags were still in the car. I unfolded the English speaking morning newspaper just as the waitress appeared. She took my order and left. As I was leafing through the paper I didn't notice that the map had slipped out of my back pocket onto the floor. Absorbed in the sports page, I wasn't aware of Maria standing there until she tapped me on the shoulder. Startled, I looked up to see her smiling, holding the map.

"Excuse me, you dropped this," she said.

"Oh thank you very much."

"Are you touring the area sir?"

I wondered if everyone in Europe spoke English.

"Why yes, but I am staying here for a few days."

"That's nice," she said while returning to her table.

I hesitated for a few minutes, not being able to concentrate on the paper.

Maria poured some more tea, added sweetener and with a long sigh, stretched, and looked out at the panorama of the countryside. She had no plans for today, and that was fine with her.

The waitress returned with my coffee, a basket of hard rolls, fresh butter and marmalade. I was trying to focus on the newspaper when she brought a warm plate, cold cuts with meat and cheese, and an insulated basket with soft boiled eggs. I looked at the eggs and the egg cup, not knowing what to do.

Maria was watching me, and laughed, "May I show you?"

I looked around while she approached my table. She placed an egg in the cup and deftly cracked open the top. "Now all you have to do is either use your spoon or dip your bread in the egg."

Feeling like a lummox, and stammering another "thank you", I said, "are you from here? Would you like to join me?"

"I don't want to bother you."

"Please, maybe you can tell me some things about the Village and the Castle."

"I would be happy to join you. Let me get my tea."

David stood up and pulled out the chair facing him. She placed her cup on the table and sat down. "My name is David Schilling. I am from Ohio in the United States."

"I knew you were an American. I am Maria Albrecht. I live in Munich but my home was from near here. How long are you staying in Bavaria?"

"I will be here until Sunday of this week. Maria: that is a pretty name."

"It's a stage name and my middle name. My real name is Heide Maria Albre-cht."

"Oh, are you an actress?"

The man from the Castle approached the table, just as she was about to answer. "Sir, pardon me, I don't want to rush you, but I have to leave for the Vil-lage to pick up some supplies. I will be able to show you the rooms before I go."

I looked at Maria, "Well—I." "Oh please don't let me keep you. I will see you here this week," she said.

CHAPTER 7

▼

THE CASTLE, 2001 LOTAR HERRON

Lotar Herron introduced himself as owner of the Castle Inn and manager of the historic site of the adjoining medieval Castle built by a Count in 1,100 AD. The Count's descendents, in fact, still owned the large estate, including the adjoining forest. Lotar was a big man, broad shouldered, with a full head of bushy grey hair and a full, but well trimmed, beard.

As we proceeded up the staircase to a dark hallway, he gave me a short history of the Village, the Castle and the Count. At the top of the stairs he turned on the lights, to reveal a long corridor with doorways to rooms on either side. In the middle of the corridor was a larger entranceway with carvings and designs that looked more like an outside entrance than a room entrance. I wondered what that was but didn't ask. At one end of the corridor was another larger door. There was a pool table and a ping pong table in a wide spot at the middle of the corridor with stuffed sofas around it.

Something about the corridor made me feel uneasy even though the lights were on. This feeling went away when he showed me the first room with high ceilings, and a huge feather bed. The room overlooked the arbor and the same pastoral scene of the countryside.

"The person in the poster for the opera in Munich looked a lot like you," I said.

"Yes that is me. My wife and I are in the theatre and have been for many years. We keep the Inn for a retreat. Our caretaker is on vacation. We take this time every year to operate the Inn for two weeks."

After a few more exchanges of information, I finally asked, "I saw the entranceway in the corridor with the carvings and all the stonework. I just wondered what that was, since it is so different from the other room entrances."

"Oh you mean the medieval castle. Come I will show you."

I followed him to the door. He took a huge key from his pocket, opened the heavy door, walked in, and said, "Come in."

I walked through the door onto a landing and then stood still, in shock, at the scene in front of me.

CHAPTER 8

▼

THE VATICAN
INFORMATION, 2005
NANCY REILLY,
MONSIGNOR AVERTI

Nancy Reilly sat down in her chair, while listening to Monsignor Dominick Averti. When he finished speaking she said, "Monsignor, would you mind if I place my phone on its hands free mode so that I can take notes while we are talking?"

In his rich baritone voice he said, "Certainly, Nancy, but please call me Dominick."

"Yes Dominick, but you must know that I feel slightly uncomfortable in using your first name. You see, I want to plan a trip to Rome, to visit you, with your permission, and to follow up with your offer to take me into the Vatican archives."

"Of course, Nancy; when will you arrive?"

She saw from the display that another message had just arrived in her voice mail.

"I am not exactly sure, but I am planning eight to ten weeks from now depending upon your schedule. I am hoping to go to the Louvre in Paris to study some of the Da Vinci paintings hanging there within the same trip."

"What a coincidence," he said, "I must be in Paris in June to meet with a university group. Perhaps we can arrange to arrive at the same time."

She had that strange flushing feeling again and could feel her face grow warm.

"I, I, would like that," she said, with a slight stutter.

While they were finalizing their arrangements Nancy was thinking about why she was so flustered around the Monsignor. Had she always been attracted to men that were somewhat unattainable? In high school in Indiana she had opted to continue with the women's basketball team and her infatuation with tennis. She had to pass up the urging by the cheerleader's coach to try out for that squad but she did finish her senior year with academic honors and as homecoming queen. She had a crush on one of the married teachers and could do little to conceal it. He finally touched her after a close encounter at adjoining lockers, at the back of a classroom, after all the other students left. There was no mistaking the positive vibrations between them. She was beautiful, gifted, and very mature for her age. He was handsome, athletic, but married with a two year old daughter. His wife was a charmer, very outgoing with a perpetual smile. He, however, was only human, and could not help noticing her, even though he knew the potential danger. She was backing out of her locker and turned to come face to face with him.

In her surprise she moved quickly and her breasts brushed against his arm. He placed his hand on her shoulder; she said, "Oh I am sorry," but it was too late. A force caused them to embrace. Then he stepped back and said, "Oh my God! What am I doing?"

"It's okay", she said.

"No it's not. Please forgive me." He rushed out of the room.

Thinking back over the episode and the encounters that followed, she missed the Monsignor's question. "Nancy, are you there?"

"Oh yes, I am sorry, I was distracted by someone coming into my office. Those dates will be fine. I will verify my flights and call you right away to confirm. It is so nice to hear your voice."

CHAPTER 9

▼

OPUS DEI HEADQUARTERS, NEW YORK 2005 GUIDO

"Guido, step in quickly!" The dark featured man moved his heavy frame through the doorway and set the heavy bag on the floor. He kneeled and reached for the Bishop's outstretched hand to kiss his ring. "I am honored to be here your eminence."

The room was obscure, located in the center of the forty story building, behind heavy equipment in the mechanical room. No one had any reason to be in this area except the licensed engineers, with credentials and the key pass cards to enter. There was a hidden entrance through the walk in closet in the Bishop's living quarters, adjoining his office. No one was aware of this entrance other than the Bishop. The only other persons coming to the room had to arrive through a service elevator that had no scheduled stop on this floor. They had to go to the floor above and walk a flight of stairs to enter.

Guido's long limousine ride from Washington D.C. had been uneventful. He had slept most of the way and arrived refreshed, ready for his duty assignment.

The room was well lighted revealing the massive amount of computer and communications equipment. The tower on top of the forty story building completed the private satellite system. Joseph, a former NASA engineer, and current member of the National Security Agency, was in charge of all transmissions from the command center. A spy system could intercept and record telephone and email conversations from anywhere in the United States and Europe, as well as providing private communications to almost any place on earth.

Guido, sighed deeply when left in his very small room, just large enough for a bed and dresser. There were no windows. "Wait here until the others are assembled," said the Bishop after showing Guido to his room. There was a pitcher of ice water, and some fresh snacks lying out on the dresser. Although mentally weary from all his travel and the gravity of his assignments, he was grateful to be here and to serve the Bishop and the Opus Dei. He did not realize that his commitment was a form of fanaticism, but believed that he truly was doing God's work and was willing to sacrifice anything for his promised rapture in eternity.

Although he was not privileged to know the Bible, he was aware that other people's deaths must occur in God's plan, just as happened to Jesus Christ. He was on his knees praying when he heard the soft tone of a doorbell and looked up to see the green light over his doorway, signaling that he was to come to the assembly room.

His childhood had been in Sicily, where he was trained by his uncles in espionage and the art of killing enemies of the family and the church. He was raised by his grand mother, after his father was murdered, and his mother's early death from child birth. Schooled only in the church, his faith grew to fanaticism. At the age of twelve he was sent to family in Northern Italy, just a few miles from the Austrian border. He became a handy man for a Catholic school and was taught to speak fluent German. At age sixteen he was taken to the Abby at Etal in Bavaria and at nineteen was smuggled into the United States to an affiliated Benedictine order, the St. Bernard Abby in Alabama. With intense training in English and forged documents he became a citizen of the United States.

Guido entered the large assembly room where the Bishop and eleven other men were waiting. There were electronic maps on the walls displaying locations of the operatives for the organization and targets for surveillance. The area containing the computers was staffed by technicians busy at work. It seemed as if they were traveling inside a giant space ship.

A short Mass was performed and then the assembly was broken down into groups of three. The leader of each of these groups then extracted vows of loyalty to the Opus Dei and the pledge to carry out their assignments. Guido was assigned to follow David Schilling and Nancy Reilly. Another was given Dr. Trent Warren at Columbia University.

▼

THE MEDIEVAL CASTLE
2001 DAVID, LOTAR

David stood speechless looking at the scene before him. At the bottom of a long flight of stone stairs was a huge room with a ceiling thirty feet high. At the end of the room, windows from floor to ceiling were almost covered by draperies but a sliver of sunlight shone through highlighting a beam of dust particles. There was enough light to see the center area while the walls were only partly visible. A huge stone hearth and fireplace was to the right. Suits of armor and implements of war and torture were scattered about the outside. Hunting trophies adorned the walls. The stone floors were covered by a huge rug in the center part where a large wooden table and chairs were placed. It appeared as if a banquet had just happened here. The table was set with candelabras, plates, and vessels for serving wine. Sofas were placed about the outside of the room.

David immediately thought of the old Count Dracula horror movies he had seen as a child. The tapestries depicted hunting, battle and torture scenes. It appeared as if someone had just closed the door on the scene a thousand years ago and could start it all back in motion with the flip of a switch.

Lotar broke David's concentration, "You have probably heard of these castles in your history books."

David trying to gather his thoughts said, "Well what is this place?"

"This Hall is the remaining part of the castle. The rest was destroyed in a battle with warring tribes. The Count and his family have preserved this for centuries, and later built the modern part of the Castle that is now being used as an Inn."

David saw a painting, with men dressed for battle, which resembled ones of the Knights Templar that he had seen in text book photos. The cross was of even dimensions like the flag of Switzerland and not the traditional cross that is used in churches.

"This is remarkable," David said, after clearing his throat. "Are we allowed to go down into the Hall?"

"Normally, no, but on special occasions I have taken people in there."

"Mr. Herron I know that this is a lot to ask but perhaps if you know of my background and credentials, I could prevail upon you to see the room. You see I have traveled extensively and am in the process of writing a book about history, especially from the beginning of the Christian religion and the effect that the dark ages and the reformation had upon our churches. This castle is like a step back into that medieval time period."

Lotar began to turn to the door and said, "Let me think about your request. I need to get to the village now and to lock this place."

David moved into his room and unpacked. Then he went back to the garden to finish his breakfast. By the time he returned Maria Albrecht was gone.

CHAPTER 11

▼

DOMINICK AVERTI AT AGE THIRTEEN 1968

"Dominick, come in here, now!" His mother was standing at the doorway impatiently waiting. "Yes mother, I am coming," he said, obediently, smiling. As he ran across the soccer field, the wind was blowing his dark curls, and she could see the mud and scrapes he had collected from the game. The others stood dejected watching him leave. Without Dominick's skills his team had little chance to win.

"You must get bathed and dressed for church," his mother said in a slightly scolding but very fond voice.

"Yes mother; do I have time to eat?"

"I have laid food on the table. You can eat as soon as you are finished dressing."

Dominick was large for his age, at thirteen. Growing up in the protective monastery environment, his education in the Catholic religion and his other studies were intense. He did all his duties: studying, playing, work and devotion to his mother with enthusiasm and joy. The monks were grooming him for the priesthood and were pleased with his academic prowess. The girls in the village, young and older, could not take their eyes off him, with his dark curly hair and penetrating brown eyes. His father died when Dominick was only four, so he was raised by his mother and the members of the order. All were very fond of him.

The Holy Father in charge of the monastery could see a bright future for him because of his intellect and his charm. It took all the political ingredients to advance towards leadership and possibly a place in the Vatican.

The young woman watched Dominick as he entered the church. She was fifteen with green eyes with red hair. When he had finished the services she was waiting for him. "Dominick, she said smiling, could you walk home with me? I am afraid of the dark street and the stray dogs."

Even with their age difference, he was about a half head taller than her. There was a chill in the air from the snow capped mountains in the background. Noticing her shiver, Dominick pulled Angelina's sweater over her shoulders. He was aroused by her closeness as she leaned into him. At her front door, the narrow street was deserted, except for a stray dog sniffing at garbage near the curb.

"I am not sure anyone is home. Could you come in with me to help with the lights?"

"Sure, he said, but I have only a minute. I must get to my studies to be ready for the examinations tomorrow."

She tried to reach a lamp high on the wall but couldn't. "Here, let me help you." he said.

She turned to speak to him but embraced him instead. Dominick was, of course, inexperienced with women, but he found himself erect. They kissed with such passion that they were in her bed before either could hesitate. The first time at making love for either of them was like an earthquake. Afterwards she had tears in her eyes and he was so embarrassed that he apologized and ran home.

"Father, I have sinned." Dominick's eyes were tightly closed and his fists clenched in anguish. The priest calmly extracted Dominick's confession and prescribed the penance for the young man.

The ascension of Dominick through schooling, priesthood, advanced degrees and research was truly remarkable and one that was followed and guided by important persons in the church. He could not know what role was in store for him when he began his apprenticeship in the Vatican, nor did he know that he left the seed of a child behind him.

CHAPTER 12

▼

WASHINGTON, D.C., MAY 2005 DAVID, NANCY

"Hello is this Ms. Reilly?"

"Yes, this is Nancy; may I help you?"

"This is David Schilling. I met you at the library and you gave me a ride back to my hotel."

"Oh yes David, I remember. How is your research going?"

"Fine; I wondered if you would be willing to have dinner with me to discuss the ideas you mentioned to me when we met?"

The Prime Rib on K Street is a hang out for politicians, actors and sometimes high class hookers. The food, especially the steak and prime rib, is outstanding. David stood up as the waiter escorted Nancy to the table. He had already ordered a martini. She was wearing tweed slacks with a black turtle neck sweater that highlighted her blond hair. Her smile and the most gorgeous blue eyes just about wiped him away.

"It is so nice to see you," she said as she shook hands with him. His palms were moist in anticipation and the excitement of seeing her. She had been in the fore front of his mind for the past several days.

"Thank you for meeting me Ms. Reilly."

"Please call me Nancy."

"Of course, Nancy. Would you like a drink or should we order a bottle of wine?"

"What are you drinking David?"

"Oh, a vodka martini. I allow myself only two of these on occasion."

"That sounds good. I'll have the same thing."

The waiter turned to speak to a co-worker while the bartender finished the drinks and placed them on the tray. It was so busy and noisy in the bar that no one noticed the dark featured man drop a small capsule in each drink. He had come here to watch Nancy and David after eavesdropping on their phone conversation by a relay from the headquarters.

By the time the drinks arrived at the table, David and Nancy were engaged in animated conversation about their research projects.

"Strange things have been happening for the past several weeks," said David, slightly lowering his voice.

"What do you mean David?"

"I don't know, maybe it's my imagination. Trent Warren, my friend at Columbia University, was working with me on my project, but when I went to see him he had received threatening messages by phone and at his desk, warning him to stop working with me. And then I have this feeling that I am being followed."

Nancy's composure took a serious turn while she listened. After a hesitation she said, "This is really odd. I have had some of the same experiences. My daughter, Ruth, called me almost in hysterics, to tell me that she had received an anonymous phone call warning her that I could be in danger if I continue to pursue my research about the lost books of the bible. Then my former husband called with the same message. They knew about my plans for a trip to the Vatican. I don't know how that could be. I have told no one except Monsignor Dominick Averti, whom I plan to visit there."

David sipped his drink after joining Nancy in a toast, then, with a serious look said, "Do you think these are just coincidences from a crank caller?"

Before she could answer, the food arrived and they began to eat. While they were finishing dinner, David said, "I can have the waiter call for a taxi to drop you off at your apartment and me at the hotel." Would that be all right with you?"

"That would be fine David," she said as she put her hand to her fore head. "Do you think it is warm in here?"

By the time they arrived at Nancy's apartment building David was feeling warm and dizzy. Nancy looked at him, "Are you okay?"

"Yes, I think so but those drinks were powerful. I just feel a little faint."

"David I hate to leave you here like this. Why don't you come up to my apartment until you feel better? I can fix us some coffee and then call another taxi when you are okay."

"Well I hate to be an imposition but I really don't feel too well."

By the time they sat down in her living room, Nancy was also feeling dizzy.

They woke up six hours later, both on the living room sofa. Her apartment had been searched.

Guido had entered her apartment after expertly picking the lock. Nancy and David were sprawled on the sofa. He searched her apartment thoroughly and opened her computer. With the latest in hardware devices he downloaded the entire contents of her hard drive. He walked back through the living room and while looking at them and thought, *it would be so easy to kill both of them now, but I have specific orders to leave them unharmed.*

He then went to David's hotel room and downloaded the contents of his laptop computer, after searching the room.

"Ms. Reilly, are you sure no one has a key to your apartment?" the detective said.

"No one except my daughter," she said. Nancy had a splitting headache. David was in her bathroom taking a shower to help his recovery.

After the detective completed his questioning and left, David came out of the bathroom, refreshed. Nancy was just sitting there in shock. She looked up at him, breaking the trance, and brightened slightly, "We have known each other only a few hours but I feel we have had experiences of a life time."

"I am so sorry all this happened. I know you must get to work. Nancy, I will call you, if you like so we can try to find out what or who is following us?"

CHAPTER 13

▼

THE CASTLE, NEAR THE ABBY OF ETAL, BAVARIA 2001, DAVID, MARIA

David sat motionless in the darkness. His laptop computer went blank and the room lights went out. Puzzled, he found his suitcase and the flash light he always carried when he traveled. He looked outside and all the lights were out. He went to his room door to look into the hallway just as Maria opened her door with a candle providing the only light from her room.

"Are you okay?" he said. "What happened?"

Maria walked into the hallway, "I guess we lost the electricity. It is so dark and scary here."

He approached her, "Let's go to the desk, maybe they know what happened."

The storm with sheets of rain, lightning and thunder was raging outside.

"Here hold onto my arm. We have plenty of light with my flashlight."

She was shivering when she grasped his arm. The hallway was spooky and silent. As they proceeded towards the end a sliver of light was visible from the same entrance that led to the medieval castle. He paused and they stood there.

"There seems to be something happening in there. Hold on let's look."

Maria grasped his arm even tighter. He pushed open the door to hear chanting and see candlelight for some kind of ceremony taking place. There were men in costumes moving about the room. Just as they stepped forward a man approached them from the rear and grabbed them both by the arm. He was carrying a huge sword, a big man with a very menacing look. He pushed them onto the landing and closed the heavy door behind them.

The sentinel had left his station momentarily to look out at the lightning. On the inside of the medieval castle, with the stone construction and the massive drapes pulled tightly closed, there was no perception of the storm. The ceremony was being conducted entirely by candle light. Before two other men arrived to restrain them, David had a faint recollection of the similarity of this ceremony and one in which he had participated at another time.

The sentinel left their side, walked down the stone stairway, and approached the leader with a sign that was promptly returned in recognition. The leader looked up at David and Maria and beckoned the other guards to bring them in front of the meeting.

"Why have you entered this hall without permission?" Even though his face was hidden by his hooded cloak, there was something familiar about his voice. The other participants stared and edged closer creating a very menacing feeling.

In the background David could see the painting with the Knights Templar wearing a uniform displaying the red cross. There was a copy of Leonardo Da Vinci's painting of the last supper. The candlelight shone directly on the person to Jesus' right, who was being threatened by one of the disciples. There were documents on the big table and ancient bound books.

"I, I, am sorry. The storm knocked out the lights and we were trying to find someone who could help us."

"Seize them and bind them," the big man said in German. David and Nancy were escorted roughly into another room, where they were bound and blindfolded.

After a few minutes had passed three men in costume entered the room. "You are American, No?"

"Yes," said David. "I am sorry. What have we done?"

"You have intruded into a meeting for which you could be killed."

Maria gasped in German, "Oh no! Please! We did not mean to enter this room. It was a mistake."

"Keep them bound until we bring the Master here."

The Master entered the room, grasped David by the hand, and pulled him to his feet. Something clicked in David's mind and he and the Master exchanged embraces. Barely perceptible, they seemed to communicating with each other.

"Release him," said the Master, in German. To David in English, he said, "What do you know about her? Can you vouch for her?"

"We have only just met," said David, "but we innocently stepped in here because of the light."

The Master frowned and threw a dark look at the sentinel. "Why did you leave your post? To the other guards, he said, "Seize him. Take her into another room."

The Master sat and talked with David, his face hooded and his voice guarded. Because of David's responses, he realized that they had common backgrounds in the Masonic ritual. Satisfied that David and Maria knew nothing about the secret meeting, the Master warned them not to discuss this incident with others and ordered the guards to escort them out of the Medieval Castle. David understood that the pain of death could result from loose talk by Maria or him.

As they were leaving, David noticed that the books and documents were missing from the table top in the great hall.

The guards released them into the hallway, where they stood wondering what to do. "Maria, how do you feel? Are you okay?"

"Yes, I think so. What was going on in there?"

"It was definitely something we were not supposed to see. Let's walk downstairs and see if anyone is at the desk."

The storm was still raging outside. There was no one visible at the bar or the dining room. "Would you like to come up to my room and discuss the events while we wait for the power to come back on?"

They sat in David's room by candle light and shared a bottle of wine. "Maria, I am working on research for a book and I noticed several things tonight that I have been questioning for years. Are you Catholic?"

"No, I really haven't followed any religion for years but my mother is Protestant. Why do you ask?" She was shivering and David offered her a blanket to put around her shoulders. It was now about 11:00 PM.

"If you grew up near here, and know this area perhaps you can help me. I am meeting with someone from the Benedictine Abby in hopes of finding more information. The meeting we accidentally entered appeared to be a Masonic ritual. At first I thought we had stumbled upon some kind of Devil worship, but that was not it. The painting that showed the knight was actually a Knights Templar in battle dress. The red cross on his tunic was an early religious symbol, from before Christ."

Wide eyed, Maria said, "What were they doing in there?"

"I can only guess, but with the copy of the painting of the Last Supper being highlighted and the ancient documents and books carefully laid out on the table, it appears that they were focusing on Mary Magdalene."

"Weren't there just disciples at the last supper?"

David hesitated, "That is what we have always been led to believe. However, the painting is by Leonardo Da Vinci and his interpretation is that the person on Jesus right hand side was actually Mary Magdalene."

"How can that be? There were no women at the last supper were there?"

"It appears that Mary Magdalene was Jesus companion, was at the last supper, and was not welcomed by the other disciples. Jesus knew at that time that his death was only days from then. He introduced Mary Magdalene as the leading figure to carry on his works and to be head of the church. The other disciples were angry about this and actually threatened to kill her. It is believed that she bore Jesus child."

"But this is nothing like I have been told. Where do you get these ideas?"

David said, "The proof is the very reason I am here in Bavaria. There is told to be lost books of the Bible with a very different story than we have been taught for two thousand years as Christians."

Maria took a deep breath, "Do you mean Mary Magdalene was not really a prostitute?"

"No, the theory is that she was vilified by the other disciples to take away her power. There is strong evidence that the lost books still exist and that they have been sought by the Catholic Church for hundreds of years, and the Opus Dei, in recent history, to be destroyed."

"Why would they want to destroy the books of the Bible?"

"Think of it Maria. The Catholic Church has an enormous power base through out the world and wealth greater than can be imagined. There is evidence in history that they have killed to preserve their power."

Thinking back over this, Maria said, "If all this were true that could mean that Jesus and Mary Magdalene could actually be ancestors to people living today. What do the Masons and the Knights Templars have to do with all this?"

Just as David started to answer, the lights came on and the sounds of motors and systems returning to motion were heard in the background. A loud knocking at the door was followed by shouts, "Hello, are you all right in there? This is Lotar Herron, the manager."

I opened the door and, instantly, felt a sensation of recognition of him. "I am so sorry the lights went out. The storm momentarily caused a power interruption but I think everything is back to normal now. I tried Ms. Albrecht's door, but I see she is here with you. You two are the only guests at the Inn. Is there anything I can do for you?"

Maria asked him in German, "Do you know if we can visit the library and the archives at the Abby? Do they allow the public to go there? Mr. Schilling is doing research for a book."

When she explained what David was looking for Lotar replied, "I don't believe I would go to the Abby with that kind of request. Strange and secretive things take place there. They are not very friendly with the people of the Village. I would be very careful about talking to anyone about what you just told me."

Lotar closed the door and left abruptly. With no mention of the secret meeting, it almost seemed to David that he had not really had the experience but had a dream instead. Maria left and they both went to bed with many questions on their minds.

CHAPTER 14

▼

DAVID AND MARIA IN BAVARIA 2001, ANGELINA, BISHOP RHEIN

David woke up to sunlight streaming in the window. He stretched and walked over to look outside. The beautiful panoramic scene filled him with energy. His first thoughts were about hot coffee and then the excitement of beginning a day of searching for information.

He opened his room door to a knocking and there stood Maria. "Good morning, David. I'm sorry to disturb you."

"Well good morning, did you sleep well?"

"Yes pretty well. I woke up thinking about the village where I grew up. There is a Catholic Church and school. Even though we were not Catholic they were very kind to us. My mother still lives there. They have extensive libraries. I was just wondering if you would like to talk with the priests there to see if you could get some of the information you are looking for."

"That sounds interesting. I really have no plans until my meeting on Friday. I was hoping to spend time at the Abby of Etal but that doesn't seem to be a very good idea. Can I meet you for breakfast to make plans?"

David drove the rented car over tree lined, winding roads into the mountains. The Alpine air was exhilarating. After an hour and a half they drove into another enchanted village. Maria was excited about seeing her mother and being home.

They parked the car half on the street and half on the sidewalk. There was a small bakery on the street and a restaurant on the second floor adjacent to the Pension where Maria's mother lived and managed. There were a variety of other shops on the street level.

As they walked into the dining room the woman turned to face them. She was an older replica of Maria, with red hair and green eyes. "Oh my darling you are here," her mother said as she rushed to embrace Maria. There were tears of joy in both their eyes.

"And who is this with you?"

"Mother I would like you to meet David Schilling, an American. I met him at the Castle Inn near Etal, yesterday."

"Welcome Mr. Schilling," she said with a broad smile, "would you both like some coffee? Please sit down here. I will be right back."

The room was cheerful with the early morning sun delivering light through the stained glass windows. There were ten tables covered with fresh linen table cloths and set up for breakfast. A basket of fresh flowers stood at the entrance next to the registration desk.

"Your mother looks just like you," David said, while fidgeting with the silverware.

"Do you think so? I have been told that before. Mother has worked very hard. I never knew my father. He left the village when I was two years old."

A waitress brought a basket of rolls and fresh coffee to the table, and Maria's mother appeared carrying a tray of pastries. "Maria loves sweets Mr. Schilling. Please have some."

Her mother sat down with them, while they ate and engaged in pleasant conversation. "What brings you to Bavaria Mr. Schilling?"

"Please call me David. I am traveling to do research for a book I am writing."

"Oh, are you an author?"

"Well I hope to be," David said with a slight hesitation. I have had some poetry and short stories published, but I made my living for years in real estate."

With a smile she said, "May I ask the subject of your book, David?"

"It is based around religious history, mainly the Christian religion; and how it has affected our lives for the last two thousand years."

"My goodness that is an ambitious project. How far along are you?"

"I am about three fourths of the way finished, but I had to come to Europe to search archives in hopes of finding information about missing books of the Bible."

"Maria, it sounds as if David needs to talk with Bishop Rhein. He is very old but he has the most knowledge of the libraries at the Cathedral. I think they have ancient books, there. He certainly would talk with you, since he took so much interest in you when you were a little girl"

They checked into their respective rooms and prepared to go to the Cathedral. As they were leaving Maria's mother pulled David aside and said, "David, I hope you can find some information that you are looking for. Bishop Rhein is still friendly to me but there has been a change in the leadership at the church. The Bishop is not in charge there, but he has a lifetime of care and a home for the rest of his days. I think you can trust him but be careful who else you talk with there. Remember that we were not Catholic but that he showed us great kindness."

David started to answer but Maria came back into the hallway after buying some fresh pastries at the bakery on the street. They were to be a gift for the Bishop.

They drove a few blocks along cobblestone streets and looming in front of them was a very imposing Cathedral and compound of buildings. David was taken by surprise at the complex. There were children running about the court yard and several priests walking among them. After they parked, Maria led David to the Church office. A young woman was at the desk. When they asked about Bishop Rhein, the woman frowned, and hesitated. Then she excused herself and went to another room. When she returned she was smiling and said, "Come with me. I will take you to the Bishop."

They walked across the courtyard and into the dark corridor of one of the buildings. There were artwork and statues throughout. They walked down a flight of stairs and stopped at a wooden door. The woman knocked and after a minute or two the elderly Bishop opened the door. He stood in surprise for a moment and then said, "Maria, my dear, come in."

The Bishop's living quarters were spacious but cluttered with books. A glass door from the living room looked out onto a courtyard shaded by oak trees. A wooden desk was placed so that there was access to the book shelves and a view to the outside. After the introductions the Bishop said, "Please won't you sit down? May I offer you some tea or coffee? I don't get many visitors these days. It is so nice to see you."

The nun carried the tray to a coffee table and prepared their snacks for them. "Thank you sister," the Bishop said as she left. "They do such a wonderful job of taking care of me. Now tell me what can I do for you?" His hands shook slightly as he sipped his tea. It had been a long time since he had had a haircut. The grey hair was sticking out around his ears, but he was clean shaven and otherwise tidy. His robe had seen many years of service.

"Bishop Rhein, Mr. Schilling is working on research for a book concerning the history of religion. I just wondered if you could help him find some of the material he is looking for."

David waited patiently. "Of course, Mr. Schilling. What information do you need?"

"You see I am studying the time of Christ and the origins of the Christian religion. I am trying to summarize how the history affects our present day culture."

"I see," said the Bishop. "Is there specific information you need?"

"Well yes, sir, I have been trying to find manuscripts and information on the lost books of the Bible."

The Bishop looked up in surprise and held out his hand as if to stop David's conversation, "Lets step outside into the courtyard for some fresh air."

The Bishop was slightly unsteady on his feet but opened the door and gestured for them to step outside. "Maria, things are not the same here as when you were a little girl."

"What do you mean father?"

"The new leaders of this Church have different views about things." He spoke very softly and came close to her so she could hear. "How well do you know David? Do you trust him?"

"Well we just met, but yes."

The Bishop took Maria by the arm with David following, out away from the building, and was just beginning to talk with Maria when a nun came across the courtyard, in a hurry. "Father is this Miss Albrecht? If it is she has an urgent phone call."

Maria excused herself in surprise and went to take the call.

"Mr. Schilling I just met you but I must tell you something in confidence since I have so little time."

David looked surprised and said, "I don't understand."

"They are threatening to take me away from here. I believe that my conversations in the apartment are being overheard by those who feel threatened by my teachings of openness for the good of the Church. I must tell you something about Maria that no one knows and that could place her in great danger. I may not have much time."

CHAPTER 15

▼

WASHINGTON D.C. MAY, 2005 NANCY, RUTH, DAVID

Nancy thought back over her phone messages, the drugging incident at the Prime Rib restaurant, her plans to travel, the mysterious hang-ups and noises in the background, and the sense of being followed. What were the problems surrounding David Schilling? With the intensity of her job, her education, and her relationships she was feeling overwhelmed. Why did she have these unidentified feelings when she talked with Dominick Averti?

"Mom, what is going on with you?" Ruth said impatiently. The sidewalk café was busy with a lunch time business crowd. Ruth was chic in an orange light weight sweater with her blond hair newly cut and permed. She was carrying books for her literature and art classes.

"What do you mean, dear?"

"You are so distracted all the time. What was that anonymous threatening phone call all about? Are you in some kind of trouble?"

"Ruth, we get crank phone calls at the library periodically. Ninety nine percent of the time it means nothing."

"But Mom how did they get my phone number and Daddy's?"

Nancy felt her face grow warm and when she looked away from Ruth's demanding stare she saw a man standing on the street corner, in a crowd of pedestrians, looking at them. *Is this just my imagination? Haven't I seen that man before?*

"Mother I am frightened. Please tell me what is happening to you."

Trying to change the subject, Nancy said, "It is really nothing." "How is your school work going?"

There was a screeching of tires followed by a loud crash at the corner as two cars collided. In the confusion, Nancy noticed that the man was gone.

She felt someone tap her on the shoulder. There stood David Schilling. He was carrying a brief case and was dressed in his customary light weight summer khakis. "Nancy, I am sorry to disturb you, but I was just on the way to your library and saw you sitting here."

"Hello David. I didn't know you were in town. I would like to introduce you to my daughter, Ruth. She is a student at George Washington University."

Ruth smiled and nodded but didn't seem very thrilled with meeting anyone while with her mother.

"How do you do? Nice to meet you," David said. I am very sorry to intrude. Nancy will you be at the library later this afternoon?"

Nancy shook her head, *yes.*

"Maybe we can have a few minutes to talk, then," said David as he waved and walked away."

"Who is that man mother?" Ruth said impatiently.

The sirens for the accident and the general confusion made it almost impossible to talk and be heard. "He is just someone from the library doing research for a book," Nancy said above the noise.

David was lost in his thoughts as he entered the library.

CHAPTER 16

▼

DAVID SCHILLING AS A CHILD CIRCA 1960—YEAR 2001 BISHOP RHEIN REVELATION

Medieval torture devices David later studied couldn't have been much less comfortable than wool knickers.

Youth activities in the Methodist Church were the beginning of his spiritual self, though seriously side tracked by his mother's insistence that he sit through boring church services in these knickers with elastic bindings around the knees and the back of his legs. The wool cloth felt like a burlap sack next to his skin. Mortification of the flesh began here, in his opinion.

From the time David was a child he had been fascinated by books and reading. At first it was only frivolous reading of fairy tales, then more sophisticated children's books. There wasn't a kindergarten at his rural school but he progressed rapidly in first grade and amazed his teacher with his interest in reading. She helped him choose books and saw that he always had some to read at home.

With his mother's bed time stories, and the libraries, books became his best friend.

The elective reading process made school work easy, particularly English and literature. At Ohio State University his entrance tests allowed him to skip the remedial English courses that many entering freshman had to take.

The classics and poetry became an interest at about the time he served in the Army, after college.. His frustration was that the world was full of so much information that each new subject led to endless research possibilities.

His creativity started with projects on the farm, extended to drawing and painting, and then to writing poetry and short stories after college. The independence typical of farm kids coupled with the creative inclination led him to self employment with a career in real estate. The creation of building projects and the satisfaction of seeing them built and occupied took a lot of the energies he would have used otherwise in more writing during his early work years.

As captain of the high school football team and a starter on the varsity basketball team, along with farm work, school was secondary but fairly easy for him.

The foundation of reading and books, and later the internet, provided so much information that his natural curiosity made him want to write as an expression of his interests and philosophy.

Strangely enough his writing skills did not evolve from English and literature classes but from a course in business letter writing at Ohio State. The instructor was brutal in red lining his letters with hackneyed phrases and clichés. From this he began to learn what he wanted to say in fewer words. Compliments along the way, "you write well," only fueled the fire to write.

A few poems were published and several short stories were written but never sent any where. He began to struggle for writing time each day along with the demands of his business.

The Alanon, Twelve Step, program allowed him to look at the world differently, to give up the need to control everything in his universe, and to listen more intently.

His experiences and interest in women were intense, but sporadic, in that his interest easily waned in relationships after a short time. It seemed that when he finally reached his goal he felt it was time to move on. This was not a happy experience in many cases. The young girls, in his high school days, were great at teasing but with their puritan training, forced most healthy young men on the path to masturbation.

While David was fairly successful at self analysis, he could not explain his quest to spend time alone, and to be at ease with his own company. It some cases, this did not lead to good social experiences. Instead of being a "groupie" he was more likely to be described as a "loner".

Brief experiences in theatre at high school Dramatics Club, class plays, and in the Theatre Department at Ohio State aroused his curiosity about acting and writing. He was satisfied with his real estate career but often fantasized about an education in English, and creative writing, and the life of an author or actor.

Now here he was in an alpine village, in Bavaria, with conflicting secrets of history being revealed to him in desperation by a Catholic Bishop.

Bishop Rhein pulled David under a tree with surprising strength. He moved closer only a few inches from David's face. David could feel his warm breath and sense the anxiety. Though David had a natural tendency to resist someone entering his private space, he stood firmly and listened.

"Young man, I have only a few hours, if that, before they take me away from here. I must tell you some things and trust you. There are no other alternatives for me. I can only hope your relationship with Maria will help protect her and insure your secrecy. She and her mother are in great danger. I know things about them that even they don't know." His agitation and trembling increased as he grasped David's shirt to pull him closer. "What I am going to tell you could change the course of history."

CHAPTER 17

▼

THE ALPINE VILLAGE, BAVARIA 2001, DAVID, MARIA

.

The short drive back to the Pension with Maria was quiet and conversation was strained. "What was the mysterious phone call? How did they find you at the Church?" David was feeling stressed with the information from Bishop Rhein.

Maria was quiet and distracted after they were forced to leave quickly from the Church. The phone call, while with Bishop Rhein, was from her mother with the warning: "Maria, how well do you know David Schilling? He is being followed and is in some kind of trouble."

"What do you mean Mother? How do you know this?"

"There was this man on the telephone. I think it was a man, but the voice was disguised and guttural. He said, Tell Maria to stay away from David Schilling. He is a fugitive and could place her in danger. Powerful people want him to leave the country and will stop at nothing to see him leave. She must not tell him about this phone call or she could be killed."

Maria did not know how to respond to David's questions and tried to evade him by changing the subject. They finished the drive in absolute silence. When they arrived she opened the car door and with a forced smile, partly hidden by her sun glasses, she said, "David, it has been wonderful meeting you but I think you will have to drive back to the Castle without me. I must spend some time with my mother. I will come back there by train to pick up my luggage."

She turned and ran up the stairs without waiting for David to answer. He stood there perplexed, not knowing what to do next.

▼

CHAPTER 18

THE CASTLE, VILLAGE, ABBY OF ETAL 2001— DAVID'S MEETING WITH OTTO HEINLIN. MARIA TURNED AWAY.

The switch-back turns out of the mountains had kept David's mind occupied. The wind flowing through the windows and sun roof blew his hat into the back seat but he was almost oblivious to this while subconsciously enjoying the pastoral countryside and the rolling hills. Pre-occupation with his conversation with Bishop Rhein, and decisions about his agenda, while waiting for his Friday night meeting with Dr. Otto Heinlin, left his complete recollection of the drive back to the Castle in a haze.

———

Maria went back to the Cathedral to talk with Bishop Rhein. 'I am sorry but Bishop Rhein is no longer residing here," said the receptionist. She turned to walk away.

"But he was just here a few hours ago. Where has he gone?"

"I do not have that information. Please excuse me."

"Who is in charge here? Is there someone else I can talk with?"

The receptionist said, tightly with a frown, "you must leave here, now, and not disturb us any more." With that she left the room.

———

In a dark corner of the bar at the Castle, Otto Heinlin saw David, after scanning the room. The sun had just lowered over the horizon to usher in the soft hues of dusk. David rose to greet him. Maria had not been at the Inn all week after stopping to pick up her luggage. David had been out visiting churches and libraries for two days. Coincidently it was Friday the 13th, a date made significant by Pope Clement V and French King, Phillip the Fair, in 1307. All the Knights Templar were arrested, and then subjected to torture and execution.

In response to an unusual handshake, Otto Heinlin said, "have you traveled?"[1]

"Yes I have traveled, Hiram."

"Let us talk outside in the courtyard where we won't be overheard."

David followed Otto to a table away from other diners. Before being seated, Otto embraced David and they engaged in a secret communication.

"How did you find me at Etal Abby Mr. Schilling?" They were sitting at a table away from the other diners. A candle in the middle of the table, reflected off the starched white table cloth. David waited while the waiter brought silverware and goblets of ice water for each. The table was slightly off balance because of the uneven patio stones.

---

1. *Traditional greeting of recognition by Masons.*

"Dr. Trent Warren told me about your retreat at the Abby because he knew I was coming to Europe for research."

"He could have placed me in danger!" Dr. Heinlin frowned as he took a sip of water."

The waiter returned, "Would you like some of our local wine?" He described the types and they each ordered. A bus boy brought hard rolls and butter.

"I apologize for any inconvenience," David said while buttering a roll. "Trent Warren and I have been friends since the time we were in the Army together."

Warming up slightly, Otto said, "Dr. Warren gave me the information allowing me to enter the Abby for a retreat. I felt uncomfortable there and I saw some things that I was not supposed to see." He took a drink of his red wine. "This is an excellent wine, fresh, with just the right taste of the grape."

"Since you have revealed your background in the Masonic lodge to me, can we speak openly?" David pulled his chair closer.

"Yes, it doesn't appear that any one can over hear us here." Heinlin was dressed in conservative clothing with black square toed shoes and a light sweater, against the slight chill in the night air. Fashion did not seem to be an issue with him.

"Two very strange things have happened to me here, this week," said David in a low voice. Otto looked at him intently.

"First, do you know any thing about Lotar Herron, the manager of this Inn?"

Otto didn't respond but there was a hint of recognition.

David went on, "Bishop Rhein at the cathedral in the Alpine Village, told me some astounding, if not outrageous things."

"Can you be more specific?" said Otto, as he brushed the bread crumbs from his beard.

Just then, music started inside the dining room, with a piano and cello, and Lotar Herron began singing an operatic song.

"I met a young woman, here, at the Inn, earlier this week." David raised his voice slightly to be heard over the music.

Otto seemed distracted, "Perhaps we should wait until after the singing to discuss this."

After the waiter returned with the food, David began eating his veal, with a look of satisfaction on his face. Otto was busily eating in European fashion with the fork in his left hand and the knife in his right. David admired the obvious gusto that Germans exhibited at meal time.

The music finished and there was polite and enthusiastic applause from the diners. Lotar took his bows and left the dining room.

Otto paused looking at David as a signal to resume the conversation. David began, "As I said I met this young woman, an actress, here at the Inn this week. I told her about my research and the book I am writing about the history of Christianity. She took me to meet her mother at the alpine village and then to the Cathedral, there, to speak with a Bishop Rhein."

Otto focused more intently at the mention of Bishop Rhein.

"He is a more liberal member of the Catholic Clergy. He told me that he had fallen out of favor with the governing body of the Church because of his outspoken views. He seemed very frightened and confided in me that he might be taken away from the cathedral very soon."

"What liberal viewpoint was he speaking of," asked Otto.

"He was telling me about the history of the Church and the extremist measures taken over the centuries to conceal the truth about Christ, Mary Magdalene and the Bible. Then he went on to tell me about unpublished books of the Bible, and the locations of secret archives with documents that have been hidden for hundreds of years, since the crucifixion."

Otto sat back in his chair and when David paused, he said, "How did this information coincide with your research?"

"It is amazingly similar. What I don't understand is that biblical information seems readily available wherever I go. Why haven't others put all the facts together about the history and made the conflicting views public?"

Otto straightened in his chair and said," Others might not be able to travel about as freely as you. And then there is the fact that most religious disciplines have a bias all of their own. So the search for historic information is for a specific purpose. The information that doesn't meet their objective is either discarded or destroyed. It's all about power. Your research may be more objective based on truth and not a pre-determined outcome."

"I agree," David shook his head, sat back and sighed, then reached for his wine glass. He thought for a moment and then said, "His ideas about the descendents of Christ and Mary Magdalene are the most startling. He actually believes he knows the identity of one of these women. This revelation came to him while he was doing an internship at the Vatican in his youth. He has been carrying these secrets all his life."

"Did he tell you of the identity of this woman?"

"Yes he did," David said with resignation. "But for her safety I swore not to reveal her name."

Otto gave David a very piercing look, "What if others know of her identity? How is concealment protecting her? Other forces might be looking for her right now with the idea of killing her. If she doesn't know how can she protect herself?"

David looked at Otto for a long moment. "You are probably right. If I give you that information doesn't that also place you in danger?"

"You know from the secret we share that I can be trusted. Don't you realize that I have devoted my life to uncovering and revealing the wrongs of the Church?"

"All right; I will tell you but you must first promise to share your research and your theories with me."

Otto extended his hand across the table in the secret handshake and said, "That is a promise. I will tell you a few things tonight, in exchange for her name, and then we can meet in the morning and go for a walk away from crowds, where we are sure we won't be overheard."

A dark figure, in the shadows, just outside the patio wall was concentrating intently with the latest in directional listening devices, to every word being said.

Exhausted from the long week, Otto and David each went to their rooms early for a good nights sleep. In his excitement, after the information he had received from Otto and the anticipation of tomorrow's news, it took David a while to fall a sleep.

CHAPTER 19

▼

SANTA FE, NEW MEXICO 2005 NANCY'S

WILDERNESS EXPERIENCE

Nancy had left Washington in the middle of a chaotic schedule to spend a few days in Santa Fe. Her assignment, there, at the University, and some of the questions generated by readings of her favorite western authors, about this area of the West, were compelling enough to justify the break. Besides that she was a natural adventurer and her curiosity about the desert, the mountains, and the mysterious legends of the spirit world propelled her outside the confinement of her work and study program.

The snow flakes were floating uncertainly through the shafts of sunlight as if intruding where they didn't belong. Nancy, sitting outside her charming little casita, was watching the snow collect on the walled-in veranda, where two days ago she was basking in the sunshine, with a glass of merlot and a rather stale cigar.

People look at me strangely when I have a cigar, but I don't care. This is better than a three pack a day cigarette habit abandoned three years ago. An occasional cigar eases the nicotine craving.

The weather in this mountainous area changes from hour to hour, with seventy to eighty degree temperatures one day, then snow and freezing the next. At 7,500 feet above sea level the clouds roll over the mountains and across the high desert, quickly, without much warning.

She looked back inside the glass French doors at her laptop computer, the desk strewn with papers, and the fire in the little adobe fireplace. She sighed while savoring the solitude from her busy schedule and the chance to write and collect her personal thoughts.

The only intrusion was her mistake in turning on the television and seeing the news about the Gulf War in Iraq. She thought, *if we are at war tomorrow and not at war today; I wish I could reverse the sands of time, pour them back into the upper chamber of the hour glass, and put things back just the way I want them.*

Since arriving in Santa Fe, her studies in the area, and her meetings at the State Capital revealed a great deal about the demographics of the New Mexico high desert.

What have our wars proven? Ask the Native Americans, the Mexicans, the Spanish, the Germans, and the Jews who have settled this mountainous area with its unforgiving terrain and climate. At times they were actively and with innovation killing each other.

Not one of these groups has a right to the franchise, nor have I seen one with superior claim over the other, or proof that their respective dominance in time was the lasting or necessarily the correct one.

She thought back over her hike, eighty miles, north of the City, at Ghost Ranch. Yesterday she had been discontent with writing and decided to venture into the desert. During the drive in her little under-powered rental car, her thoughts drifted back to some of her readings about spirituality, the coincidences in her life, and her quest to understand the movement between the present and the next dimension. Some very prolific authors see the desert and the mountainous areas of the West as a stepping off place into the spirit world.

The escape to New Mexico came about because of her invitation to lecture at the University in Santa Fe. This was a needed departure from her busy work and academic schedule in Washington D. C. The references to the "Native Indian population", here and in other parts of the United States were observed by her to be short sighted and inaccurate. Who, in fact, were the original settlers of this land? When did they arrive? In her travels she found similarities in customs, rituals, references to the sun and moon and the ocean tides, in objects of worship throughout the world. Pyramids, for example were not found only in Egypt, but in Mexico, Central America and other parts of the globe.

The inclination for man to point objects to the heavens either to send or receive divine communication is evident in church steeples, antennas, and the growth of plants, as well as the pyramids. Where were the land bridges, who traveled them, and why? Why did some groups stay put and others continue to search and wander? How did their customs and mores eventually translate into the various civilizations of today? Why were some peoples more aggressive and dominant than others?

She thought as she drove towards the Ghost Ranch, *How can anyone be so sure of their way of life and ignore history? The richness of the secrets of the universe, yet to be discovered, gives me such vibrant interest and eagerness to greet each new day, that I can hardly wait to get started in the mornings.* The landscape was changing from wind swept desert where sage brush tumbled over the sand and soil, occasionally blowing over the roadway. Other plants clung desperately to the earth. In the distance the horizon was climbing to the alter of red mountain walls, overlooking lakes fed by melted snow.

Nancy looked down at her new hiking boots, one on the gas pedal, the other resting on the floor. Thank goodness she had thought to break them in on her daily hikes at home, and get through the blister stage, before trying them in a wilderness area. After much shopping, looking through catalogues and then talking with the footwear specialists at the outdoor store, she decided on a medium weight pair of Oslo's. Her blue jeans were faded and worn but serviceable. The sweat shirt and the rain-proof wind breaker should be just right for the weather conditions. Her blond hear was pulled back in a pony tail, in preparation for the wide brimmed hat.

As she drove into the entrance of Ghost Ranch and down the mile long driveway to the trail heads, she thought back over her early years in Indiana. From time to time she still had aching knees, one from a torn ligament and the other cartilage damage from skiing a few years ago. After the ACL incident in her teens, though, she was back on the basketball court within a week. Her mixture of beauty and brains, the outgoing personality and her athletic ability had made her like a lightning rod. Though she possessed all these gifts she carried an exterior of humility that drew people to her, young and old alike.

On the drive she had passed vast open areas dotted with mobile homes, modest ranches and shacks sheltering their owners from the desert. Interspersed were multi million dollar mansions from those who had fought the battle of the urban areas, collected fortunes and came here for solitude. Nancy wondered who had won the battle, those who stayed or those who migrated here.

A short conversation with the woman at the desk pointed her to the parking area at a trail head. She parked the car, locked her personal items in the trunk, stretched and looked around. In the distance the mixture of the red and tan stone in the mountain cliffs reminded her of the architecture of the new large Marriott hotels she had seen in Washington D.C. and other cities. Perhaps their architect was inspired by trips to the West.

She had used the bathroom at the reception center, now she put on her jacket, placed the camera around her neck and decided she was ready to hike. With the slightest bit of apprehension at her aloneness she started up the trail. Within ten minutes she was out of sight of any forms of civilization until she came upon a grave marker about thirty feet from the trail. Wondering about snakes, she walked to the grave. There were two persons buried there, apparently husband and wife, with Jewish names. She could only speculate their origin and their purpose for being there. The names did not match the name of the charitable benefactor who established the ranch.

The trail was wide at this point with mountains on both sides and rising at the front. The form of a woman at her left was silhouetted with the sun behind, seemingly sculptured from the face of the cliff and rising high above it. Could the sun and the storms over the centuries have left so perfect a figure from this pre-historic ocean bottom? She stopped and gazed up at the form perceiving a woman figure, maybe her grandmother, buxom, imposing, with her hair in a bun, then in another instant, she saw an Indian Chief with arms folded under a blanket, clearly in charge of his following. As she walked on for another ten minutes she saw plants, soil and stone formations that she was unfamiliar with, all the while with the statuesque woman figure of the mountain gazing at her.

She began to cross small streams and more rock formations and wished she had brought her telescopic walking stick with her. She took the cellular phone from her jacket pocket and opened it. There was no signal. Hmmm, *I am really all alone out here.* Some parts of the trail were becoming steep and slippery, so she looked around and found a tree branch that would do for a walking stick.

As the climbing became a little more difficult she thought back over the books she had read about persons getting lost in the desert and the mountains and the mysterious ventures into time dimensions not of this earth. Fortunately Nancy had little fear mixed with great self-confidence. On she walked.

A land slide had dumped huge boulders in the middle of the trail which had narrowed into the shallow stream bed. She was actually walking on water and had to begin climbing over the carelessly strewn rocks. As she continued upward the trail narrowed even more with the boulders becoming larger and fallen trees impeding her progress.

Looking ahead the trail was obscured by turns and the cliff's protrusion on both sides. *Am I okay with this? The sign at the trailhead said box canyon. What really is that? I have never seen one.* Her spirit of adventure over powered her caution. It now became necessary to use the make shift walking stick to keep from slipping and falling.

She stopped and looked back over the trail she had just crossed. The silence, the beauty was breath taking. She continued her climb up and over the boulders and could finally see, in the distance, what appeared to be the end of the canyon, high above her. Standing at the top of the last huge boulder, a small green meadow unfolded intersected by the shallow stream. The landscape ended directly into the sheer wall of the canyon. She looked up two hundred feet to the top thinking, *how would I ever get out of here if the trail closed behind me?*

Then she saw what appeared to be a path rising steeply and to her right. *This must be another way out. Maybe it would be easier than that climb I just completed.* She looked at her watch, *one hour and twenty minutes; I can't believe I have been out that long.* It was warm, in the sixties, but with a few snow flakes beginning to fall from the mixture of clouds and sun light.

She rested for a moment, looked back over the trail again, and started up the path. The earth under-foot caused her to slip, but with the walking stick and by grabbing bushes and saplings she was able to make her way up about half way to the top. The path turned sharply to the left and made it impossible to see the rest of the trail. There was a branch on the other side of a gap in the trail. She reached out to the branch and facing the cliff pulled her self around to a wider spot on the other side. As she looked forward the trail ended. There was no other way out.

She looked down and realized how far that would be to fall. She looked back over the gap in the trail she had just crossed and wondered how she had managed to pull herself across. She looked down again and back over the trail at the bottom. Fear visited her for a moment. *My God! If I should fall here no one would ever find me.*

With her back against the canyon wall, she looked down—a mistake; then she looked up past the rim of the canyon. There were large birds circling. Vultures? She took a deep breath and studied the gap in the trail. Then, *What the Hell, no one is going to rescue me. I have to get back by myself just like I got here in the first place.* She took a deep breath and a long step over the gap while she reached out for a root on the other side. She was safely back on the path. She stood there for a moment and looked down over the trail of boulders and slippery stream bed that brought her here. Then she side stepped down the loose soil of the slope, back to the little green meadow area at the base of the box canyon.

She stood in the meadow collecting her thoughts. *How smart was this? Two arthritic knees, one awakened from recent surgery, are laughing at my folly. They were bystanders when I leaped for a root, at a 100 foot drop off and were poised to let me down to careen over the mountainside. Sure, with the augmentation of my hands and a hastily found walking stick, the knees, fresh from two months of exercise therapy, they say, "That was fun lets do it again."*

A fallen tree trunk provided a convenient place to sit and rest for a minute. *Why am I in so many situations alone? At 49 my goals and emotions are changing. Relationships? I get so involved for a short time then I begin to see the flaws in any man. Once I win the fight for his attention or devotions or whatever, it seems that I start the process of withdrawal. Strong men, while a challenge, are shoved into the background in favor of ones I can manage and lead. What is wrong with me? Is it my age? Is it still the quest for fairy tale compatibility? The tactile physical feelings in a love relationship are thrilling and overwhelming, yet I seem to get resentful at the thought of long lasting intimacy. No one has ever really been able to explain to me the changes that my age is making in my emotional stability and the changes I am experiencing in my body. Let's face it, so many men are jerks. So are many of my women friends, I guess. Am I all alone in the world seeking both physical and intellectual companionship in the same person?*

Nancy sighed deeply and looked over the small green meadow and the boulders she would soon be crossing. This was a surreal scene as if from a Disney movie. She took a deep breath and began her descent over the steep and slippery boulders. She paused to look over the beauty of the trail in front of her and took some more pictures. At the end of the steepest part she started back over the shallow stream bed and finally got to the dry land part of the trail. By this time it was mid afternoon with the sun peeking out from the clouds, and the weather slightly warmer.

Reluctantly she discarded the walking stick that had been such a welcome companion, and walked out where the trail began to widen. There waiting for her was the chief or the maternal stone sculpture, high on a cliff, looking her way.

With the effort in her climb she had forgotten: *I did not see the Devil in the canyon, although I heard he has been here. The great chief figure governing the gate to the other side must have been on vacation, asleep or just didn't like the challenge he saw in me.*

Is the Devil just a perspective, viewed from either side, each convinced the other is he? I guess only history will tell me the true side of evil and the identity of the champion. I can only pray that if we win, that we are without demagoguery to cloud the rewards of victory.

At either the battle front or the mountainside, individuals are prepared to die, some voluntarily.

She looked back one more time before going to her car. The stone figure was still there in majesty, looking at her.

CHAPTER 20

▼

CASTLE INN—2001 MURDER

David awoke to a pounding on his room door. He had been deeply asleep dreaming a vivid scene mixed from his experiences this week and some of the recollections from the horror movies he had seen as a child.

"Mr. Schilling," a pause, then louder, "Mr. Schilling please come to the door."

"Who is it?" said David as he walked across the room.

"It is Lotar Herron. Please open the door."

Out of habit, David had bolted the door and placed a chair in front of the knob before going to bed. *That's odd, he thought, the door is not latched. I specifically remember securing that before I went to bed.*

He removed the chair and the chain, opened the door, and found not only Lotar Herron but another man and a policeman.

"What's going on?" said David, now completely awake.

He looked out into the hallway. There were several people and a gurney, with a covered figure, like a body, strapped to it.

"This is Inspector Houser of the police. He wants to ask you some questions."

They entered the room without David's invitation. "Please sit down Mr. Schilling." The Inspector was about fifty, with rimless glasses, tall and slender, with reddish hair.

"When is the last time you saw Otto Heinlin?' he said.

"Why, what is happening here?"

"Mr. Schilling Otto Heinlin was murdered some time last night. You were the last one seen with him."

"Oh my God! How—when?"

"That is what we want to ask you Mr. Schilling."

"The last time I saw him was in the patio where we had dinner. We were supposed to meet this morning to go for a hike in the forest."

"What is your relationship with Otto Heinlin?"

"I, I just met him for the first time this week. No that is not quite right, I met him years ago in Egypt."

"Mr. Schilling please describe your experiences with Heinlin."

"Well, uh, let me think. Do I need a lawyer? I am just a visitor in this country."

"Mr. Heinlin please let me assure you, your rights are perfectly protected. We are notifying the American Embassy of the incident as we speak."

"Okay, I was on vacation with my wife in Egypt on a cruise ship on the Nile river."

"When was this?" asked Houser.

"About twenty years ago."

I finished the story about the missing wallet and the short conversation with Otto Heinlin. "How did you stay in contact with him after that?'

"I never did. I never saw him again until this week."

"But you did correspond with him didn't you?"

"No, I swear," David said, feeling anger.

A uniformed policeman walked into the room and whispered to Inspector Houser. They left the room and went into the hallway.

David looked at Lotar Herron. Herron was looking out the window, careful not to make eye contact. David looked at the floor wondering where all this was going to lead.

Inspector Houser re-entered the room. Lotar and David looked at him expectantly. "Mr. Schilling, we have been in touch with your embassy. Tell us the rest of the story up until last night."

"Well I came here to talk with Otto Heinlin to get information for a book I am writing." The Inspector was taking notes, but looked up at David.

"Go on", said Houser.

David sighed, "You see Dr. Heinlin had worked with a friend of mine, Dr. Trent Warren, at Columbia University in New York City. Dr. Warren is a well known authority of religious history and anthropology. Dr. Heinlin came to Columbia to teach and to work with Dr. Warren." David paused.

Houser looked up sharply and said, "Please continue."

"When I told Dr. Warren that I was planning to come to Europe to find information from archives to investigate the missing books of the Bible, He suggested I visit Dr. Heinlin at his retreat at the Abby at Etal."

"Did you do that?" asked the Inspector.

"Yes, I did but it was only a very brief meeting. We then planned a meeting for Friday, last night, here, at the Inn."

"Who else have you talked with since you have been here in the Village?"

David hesitated, "Well lots of people. Let me think."

Inspector Houser interrupted, "Why have you not mentioned Maria Albrecht?"

"You haven't given me a chance to finish," said David, growing more irritated.

Inspector Houser's eyes narrowed and his face drew to a hardened expression. "What is your relationship with Maria Albrecht."

"There is no relationship, I just met her here at the Inn, this week."

"Mr. Schilling did you not, in fact, travel with Miss Albrecht on an over night trip to the Village in the Alps? Do you often spend the night with women that you have no relationship with?"

"Inspector, I resent your tone and your implications. I am going to refuse to answer any more of your questions until I have legal or embassy representation."

"Mr. Schilling, this is not the United States. Perhaps you do not know your rights, here, as well as you think. You are supposed to be doing research on religious history including symbology. While you are an amateur, I am told that you have become an authority on these subjects."

"Where do you get your information?" David asked testily.

Inspector Houser ignored the question and said, "Come with me. I want to show you something you might be interested in."

Houser led David to the gurney in the hallway, where a body was shrouded. He spoke to the uniformed officer, "Open the body bag and show Mr. Schilling the corpse."

David stood with officers at either side of him so that he could not step back. The policeman opened the bag. David looked, and recoiled in horror.

There was a huge wound in Dr. Heinlin's chest, where the heart would be. It was gone.

David looked at Lotar Herron. He would not meet his gaze?

Inspector Houser said, "Mr. Schilling, this appears to be a ritual murder. Perhaps you can enlighten us about the facts surrounding it."

The other officers were busy searching David's room.

CHAPTER 21

▼

THE KILLER

Guido had been careful to make no noise in the bushes as he listened to David and Otto Heinlin at their dinner table on the patio. The shrubbery just outside the wall provided a good place to hide and to use the high-tech listening device.

They finished dinner, moved their chairs back to leave, and engaged in that odd handshake, after agreeing to meet the next morning.

Guido waited for an hour, bored, but satisfied that he was doing God's work. He then entered the back stairway to the Inn at the end of the building. The thin plastic device he had placed in the door, let it appear to be closed, but allowed him to open it.

The hallway lights were low but with his map of the Inn, he found David Schilling's room. He stood outside the door with his listening device. Schilling was sleeping soundly with soft snoring. With his master key, he turned the latch and slowly inched the door forward. It stopped suddenly meeting resistance that he had not expected. He pushed harder with no results. There was no other way into the room since the only other entrance was a window, four stories above the ground.

He stopped, then muttered to himself, *It will be Heinlin's turn to die.* He went to Heinlin's room. After waiting he was sure that Heinlin was asleep. He entered the room, quietly, using the small infra red flashlight. Heinlin was lying on his back. Guido crept to the bed and placed the anesthetic mask over Otto's face. There was momentary resistance, then quiet.

Guido removed the surgical instruments from his back pack, after turning on the room lights, made his familiar communication with God, and then began his grizzly task. The saw with the power pack was very quiet. He was whistling softly while he worked.

When he was finished he went back outside the castle in the dark and made a call on his satellite phone. His instructions were to return to Washington D.C., immediately.

CHAPTER 22

▼

DAVID'S RELEASE 2001

Inspector Houser was pacing around the parking area while David was locked in one of the police vehicles. Finally, Houser could wait no longer and went back to the rooms where the forensic team was working.

"What have you found?" said Houser, impatiently.

"We were just about to come to you with our conclusions. We have searched Mr. Schilling's room thoroughly. There is absolutely no sign that he ever left his room last night."

"But are you sure? If it wasn't him then who?" His hands were gesturing impatiently as if trying to find an answer in the air. "What did you find in Heinlin's room? How did the killer enter the room?"

"This was the work of a professional. There were no finger prints and all indications were that the job was done quickly and efficiently. Mr. Schilling could not have possibly killed Heinlin, with all the mess that was made, and then disposed of all traces of evidence. There was no sign of forced entry to Dr. Heinlin's room. Either the door was unlocked or the killer had a key."

Houser sighed, "I guess I will have to release him then." *Now where do I start to find the killer,* he muttered to himself. He went to the office of the Inn to speak with Lotar Herron.

Herron looked up from his desk with a grim look on his face. Houser said, "I want you and all your staff to be available for questioning for the next two hours. I must go outside and release David Schilling, first."

Guido was on his way to the airport.

———

Maria, frightened by her mother's phone call, and the encounter with Bishop Rhein at the Cathedral, raced up the stairs at the Pension. Her mother was out. Only the cook was working in the kitchen. Maria scribbled a note and sealed it in an envelope for her mother. She hastily packed her clothes, jumped in her car and headed back to Munich. Her head was filled with fear and questions.

Just as she pulled away, the phone at the pension rang. The cook answered David Schilling's call. Finding that neither Maria, or her mother were there, he hung up and began his drive to the airport. It was time to get back to the United States to safety. Inspector Houser had reluctantly returned his passport. He needed to talk with Trent Warren and to think through all the events of the past week.

CHAPTER 23

▼

DOMINICK AVERTI—2005 VATICAN ARCHIVES— FLASHBACK

Monsignor Averti was deep in the Vatican Archives. *Alone, always alone. What have I done with my life? Have I done anything worthwhile? Are the secrets, I guard so preciously, worth guarding? Could revelations of truth turn the world further into a frenzy? My faith is solid but the more I learn the more doubt I have about man's distortion of the truth.* He was in an area of the archives restricted to only a handful of human beings. The Swiss Guard was the primary protector of the Vatican, but the clergy had the only access to the Archives.

Dominick, now in his fifties, was one of the world's leading authorities on document and archive preservation. The various types of materials used for inscription, the instability of inks, the content of the air, sensitivity to light and a multitude of other issues, including forgeries, made his line of work a rarity.

His tasks were daunting enough until he found out that he had fathered a child and had recently learned the identity. He could never contact this person because of his position in the Church. His thoughts drifted to a life outside the Church in a fantasy about family life and a normal job and home. He sighed, deeply, and continued his search for the secret passages that he suspected were hidden here. He only had so much time alone until others questioned his time in the archives. Even though he was in charge there was a strict logging in and accounting for time in the archives. This was all entered into a computer and reviewed by the assistant to the Pope.

The circumstance of his child's ancestry must be guarded by Dominick to be taken to his grave for the child's protection and for the protection of the Church. His thoughts drifted back over the years of his life. *I was so sure that a life devoted to the Church was my only option. The young woman who presented herself in the Village, early in my life, had to be an act of God. This is one of the few times I have had doubt about my calling to serve God and Man.* The code letter from Bishop Rhein had been delayed in its delivery to Dominick for almost two years. Rhein had disappeared from the Cathedral and was not heard from again.

———

Twenty five years, earlier, the secret tunnel out of the Vatican had been known to and used by only a few of the Popes in the last one hundred years. Dominick had accidentally entered it when he was working in the Pope's private quarters. The Pope had suddenly fallen ill and Dominick was summoned to stand by while the doctors arrived. His devotion even in his early twenties placed him in a position of trust inside the Vatican.

The Carmerlengo, the Pope's assistant, was operating in charge for the few days of the Pope's absence. He asked Dominick to spend a few nights in the Pope's quarters until his recovery and return. There were transition documents and artifacts that had to be guarded. Away from his normal duties in the archives, Dominick slept soundly and had time to think about his life. A vivid dream awakened him in the late evening. He paced around the Pope's quarters until he stood before a bookshelf containing volumes of history that he had never before seen.

He took one of the books from the shelf and became totally engrossed in it while leaning on a study table. He tripped over the rug on the floor when turning to replace the book and grabbed the edge of the table to catch him self. To his shock and surprise a section of the bookshelves opened wide to reveal a metal door. He stood there for a moment, and then forced the door open to reveal a tunnel. Low lighting came on automatically so that he could see part way. He knew that he was treading on sacred ground and that he should turn away, but his human instincts took over his better judgment.

It was cool and damp in the tunnel, but he was wearing street clothing with a sweater, and continued on for several hundred feet. After a few minutes he became fearful of his trespassing and about where this tunnel would lead. After about twenty minutes he came to the end. There were heavy metal doors to his left and to his right. The one on the right seemed to have a faint sound of street noise coming from it.

Dominick stood there knowing he was doing all the wrong things in his position of trust with the Church. He was, however, a young man in his twenties with all the suppressed fires of manhood in his loins. In spite of his dedication, he forced open the door that opened into an alleyway near the base of an area of ruins. He had no way of knowing that the door to the left had been used as an escape for Popes for hundreds of years. There was no conceivable reason for anyone to ever be in this area. At the end of the alley there was light and the sounds of traffic and music. The compelling attraction of the outside world was too powerful. He was in street clothing so he could walk out there and never be noticed.

At the end of the alley was a park like area with a circular street and several side walk cafes in full operation. At 10:30 P.M., in Rome, night life was just beginning. In a more secluded area, a café off to the side had tables where he could sit and listen to the sidewalk musicians. He took a table and ordered wine when the waiter came by. Fortunately he had a few Lira in his pocket.

A blond woman in a uniform was sitting two tables away, enjoying the music and her solitude. When the music stopped, she looked his way and smiled. He smiled back and then looked away. The waiter delivered a bottle of wine to her table, opened it, and poured a small amount for her to sample. Dominick could not resist looking back at her and met her gaze just as she was taking a sip from her glass.

He could not explain the feeling to himself but his temples were throbbing and he was aroused against his will. A sidewalk vendor came by with a pet ape that jumped on her table, grabbed the bottle of wine, ran to Dominick's table and handed the bottle to him. Dominick was so shocked that he was speechless. The vendor took the ape away after his apology.

The woman smiled at him. She actually was laughing. Dominick took the bottle to her table, "I am so sorry," he said.

She laughed, "It was not your fault. Thank you for returning the wine."

"Oh you are welcome," Dominick stuttered.

"Won't you sit down and join me in a glass of wine?" she said smiling.

"Oh well, I don't want to intrude, Miss."

"Please, it is a lovely evening and I would enjoy the company."

Dominick sat down and was totally tongue tied with embarrassment. He managed to say, "You are American aren't you?"

She said, "Why yes. It is that obvious?"

"I don't know, I just thought with your uniform and all."

"Yes, I am a flight attendant with American Airlines and am on a lay over here until tomorrow. I am staying in a hotel just a block from here."

Dominick was starting to regain his composure. "Have you been a flight attendant long?"

"Actually, just about a year. I have a few months left and then I go back to the University."

"Hello, I am Dominick," he extended his hand.

She took his hand and said, "What brings you to this neighborhood Dominick?"

"I am staying near here as well."

She was about to ask another question when two musicians, an accordion and a violin, walked up to their table and began play, as if they were serenading lovers.

She and Dominick looked embarrassed at the implication but smiled. When they didn't tip, the musicians went away.

They had an extended conversation while watching the lights from the boats on the nearby river. "It is such a nice night, Dominick, would I be too bold in asking you to go for a walk?"

He was completely out of control now in the presence of this lovely, engaging, blue eyed woman. "I would be happy to walk with you, although you don't know me at all."

"I have always prided myself on being a good judge of character," she said.

They walked along the river bank, and she took Dominick's arm to steady herself from her high heels. "Would you mind if I take these heels off and walk in my stocking feet?" she said.

She was diminutive and even more alluring in her shorter stature.

Dominick's senses were crashing all around him. He could hardly speak or walk straight. Any thoughts of the tunnel or the Vatican were completely gone.

They made love in her hotel room, both with the idea that they would never see each other again. When she told Dominick she was engaged and was to be married in four weeks, he was shocked but still determined that the experience was one that he could not have avoided. He left her hotel room after tearful goodbyes, and went back to the alley to the door at the entrance to the tunnel. It was locked. He had no way back into the Vatican except the front door. To make matters worse he had been locked in the Pope's quarters, and had to find a way back in there. His entire career could be ruined.

CHAPTER 24

▼

WASHINGTON D.C.,
2005—DAVID AND NANCY

"I am sorry to have intruded on the time with your daughter," David said while entering Nancy's office at the library.

"That is all right David. It is so nice to see you. It has been a while."

"How was your trip to Santa Fe?"

She looked away, "It was wonderful but I did a really dumb thing while I was there." David looked at her and waited. She told him about her hike to the box canyon at Ghost Ranch, then about her plans to visit the Vatican in Rome and the Louvre in Paris.

"You are certainly daring to attempt that hike into the desert alone. Your plans for Europe sound like a wonderful experience. I did tell you about my last research trip to Europe didn't I?"

"Yes, the Professor's death was terrible! How has your research gone recently?"

"It's interesting that you ask because I am also in the process of planning another trip to Europe. More and more questions and information about Mary Magdalene have come to light. I am going to have to go to the historical sites for authentication for my book and to be more accurate in my location descriptions."

"You had a lot of questions about the Knights Templar, David. Have you found the answers?"

"Yes, some of them but I need to go back to Germany and then to the Vatican to either complete or continue my research. It seems that every time I think I have answers, more questions arise."

"I understand, David. This is the same issue that haunts me and keeps me driving for more information. Of course, that is to be expected considering we are covering a period of history starting over two thousand years ago. I keep thinking about our current news reporting of incidents happening on a world wide basis. The accounts are so widely varied because of personal prejudices and interests that I wonder if we ever get the correct story, even with the marvelous communications system we have today. Can you imagine the confusion through the Dark Ages where books and learning had to be hidden so as not to be destroyed?"

"That very issue is the reason I am compelled to finish my book and at least expose the most truthful version to the world that I can manage," David said, sighing heavily.

"The Knights Templar issue has so many economic implications that have shaped Germany, Europe and much of the rest of the world, and the impact on governments, wars, and our social structure is virtually unnoticed."

"What do you mean David? Could you be more specific?"

"Well you remember the story about Friday the 13th in the year 1307 and the fact that Pope Clement the V and the French King, Phillip the Fair rounded up all the Knights Templars and had them killed, right?"

"Yes I remember that story."

David continued, "The reasons behind this act, and the threat that the Catholic Church felt, is the real basis of the persecution of the Templars." Nancy was focused and listening intently. "The Knights Templar accumulated enormous wealth and began the first banking system in Europe sometime around 1,100 AD. Even though they started as protectors of the Church with the blessing of the Pope, the Church eventually became jealous of their financial power. They were the warriors of the Crusades and were favored as heroes for hundreds of years. The persecution by the Church began because the Church had great indebtedness. They were forced to be dependent upon the Templar to borrow money for survival."

David paused and walked to the window of Nancy's office to look outside. It was a beautiful sunny day with lots of people walking on the streets and sitting at sidewalk cafes. He didn't really feel the ambiance of the view, but in his mind he was back in Germany at the Castle Inn and the Village in the Alps. He could not forget the ceremony and the costumes at the Castle Inn and the painting of the warrior in the white robe with a Maltese cross emblazoned on the front.

Sensing David's distraction, Nancy said, "David would you like some coffee?"

He turned abruptly, and looked at her, "Yes that would be nice."

The horror of seeing Otto Heinlin's mutilated body would stay with him forever.

David took a sip of the coffee. "Ah that is good! I like the way you make your coffee—strong."

Nancy sat back down waiting for David to continue.

He was fidgeting with his dive watch which he wore for all occasions.

"Where was I? Oh yes, the Templar banking system. They came into existence as monks, evolved into protectors for the Church, and were eventually persecuted by the Church. Those that were not killed were driven underground and actually existed as a sub-rosa organization within Freemasonry. It is said that they still exist today. During their years in favor they accumulated land and money throughout Europe. This started because they provided safe passage, in their warrior status, to travelers who needed to carry money. Eventually instead of physically transporting money or acting in the protector role, the Templar issued vouchers to travelers to be redeemed at various villages and towns in Europe. Their power grew behind the scenes to control the most powerful banking systems."

"How did Freemasonry enter into this picture," Nancy asked. "My father was a Mason."

"So am I," said David. "The ritual is very secretive. At the time I entered the lodge, the ritual seemed cumbersome and unnecessary to me. Perhaps it is in today's world, but in the reformation period, this secret society was the only way to communicate without being killed by the enforcers for the Church. Revelation of the secret ritual is threatened by death, even today. The Old Testament indicates that the necessity for secrecy began thousands of years before Christ during the building of King Solomon's Temple."

"Oh David, surely you exaggerate."

"Nancy, I think I accidentally stumbled into a secret meeting at the Castle Inn in Bavaria. Maria, the actress I told you about, and I were staying on the same floor at the Inn when the power failed during a storm. I suspect, but am not sure that the Inn Keeper, an opera singer, was in charge of the meeting. They were all hooded and in masks. There seemed to be great wealth in the background with the Inn and all the thousands of acres of forest belonging to the same owner. It certainly did not appear that the rooms at the Inn and the restaurant could have supported everything financially. Then, of course, Otto Heinlin was killed a few days later."

CHAPTER 25

▼

MARIA, BERLIN 2005

The curtain came down to thundering applause. The successful run of the play following her movie success in Europe and the United States had taken Maria's financial fortunes to a level she had never dreamed of. Everything happened so fast after her return from her encounter at the Cathedral with Bishop Rhein, that the last two years seemed like a dream. She had hardly had time to focus her curiosity upon the incident and then the news about the murder at the Castle Inn the same week. There was no more news about David Schilling and the mysterious phone call about him. *Someday, as soon as a week or two appears in my schedule, I must get back to the Village at Etal and get more information.*

On her way to the dressing room, Maria could not imagine why she was thinking about the Castle Inn in the middle of all the acclaim that was coming to her. She opened her dressing room door to be greeted by a room full of flowers and some of her faithful followers. Champagne was on ice and there was a party about to happen.

She looked around the room at familiar and friendly faces, and then she saw a man she did not recognize, a big man. *Where have I seen him before?* Suddenly the experiences in the Castle Inn at Etal and the Village Cathedral came flooding back to the forefront of her mind.

"Maria, you were wonderful; Happy birthday." She had completely forgotten her birthday because of her busy schedule. She had not even opened her mail or talked with her mother for over a week.

There were members of her cast, the producer, and a handful of friends, including her latest boy friend, Rolfe. Even though she had just turned 36 she didn't look a day over 26. As she exchanged hugs and greetings, she was smiling but still distracted by the big man standing in the back of the dressing room.

Lotar Herron had been following Maria's career from all the publicity in the news. He was concerned about the events that had happened at the Castle Inn during David Schilling's and Maria's visit, and the things they might divulge. With his status in the actor's guild, he managed to get himself invited to her birthday party.

Finally, her assistant brought Lotar to Maria. "Maria I would like to introduce you to Lotar Herron. He is currently playing in "The Student Prince" here in Berlin. He attended your performance tonight and asked to meet you."

"Miss Albrecht it is so nice to see you again. You were wonderful, tonight, and your movie was a great hit. Do you remember me from the Castle Inn in the Village at Etal?"

"Of course Mr. Herron, but I had to leave there suddenly at the end of the week I spent there."

"Yes, I know. We had such a tragedy with the death of the Professor. If you have a moment I would like to talk with you about the American David Schilling."

"I don't know anything about him, only that I met him at the Inn that week." Her assistant was tugging at her arm. "Maria, we have your cake ready and the Press is here. Could you say a few words?"

"Please excuse me Mr. Herron." Nancy said while backing away.

"Wait, Ms. Albrecht. It is very important!" He reached out as if to restrain her.

Her boy friend, Rolfe, stepped between them. "Is there something I can do for you sir?" he said in a forceful way.

The Press interviewed her and took photos. While she was busy with this and attending to her guests, Rolfe and Lotar Herron were having an animated conversation. She looked around at them again and Lotar was gone from the room.

CHAPTER 26

▼

NEW YORK 2005 GUIDO'S DILEMMA

Guido could feel himself grow rock-hard at the prospect of the two young women. Even though he was dark, he liked the red head and the blond types. His imagination was rampant with his fantasies about what he would do with them before he killed them. He was getting wet in his pants.

The electronic maps in the control room of the Opus Dei headquarters, high on an upper floor, were focused on two locations, one in Germany and one in Washington D.C. Only Guido, the Bishop, and Joseph, the electronics operator, were in the room.

There were two persons highlighted in Washington and one in Germany.

"Joseph, bring the photos and the personal data on each one of these persons to the screen"

"Yes, your eminence, which one would you like first?"

"Start with Maria Albrecht."

Joseph gave several touch commands to the computers and a life size, full figure photo of Maria appeared along with personal data imposed upon the twenty foot screen.

"Remember that as we go through these that there is a common denominator with the two women, in their backgrounds," the Bishop said in a professorial tone. "We have much research work to do to determine the exact issues. If we can't, they must both be eliminated. We have to be very careful because their deaths may be high profile but must appear accidental."

Guido was secretly distressed to hear this since it was in conflict with his fantasies.

The life size screen, with Maria, was vivid with her red hair and green eyes. She was big busted and well proportioned, even though she was not tall. There was a sexiness that radiated from her. She was smiling, with the countryside and the bright sunshine framing her beauty. Guido wanted to reach out and touch her. He had wet dreams at night but never one in the daytime. He was very close to ejaculating right now.

Her breasts were moving and her nipples very prominent in the sheer blouse. The computer operator had pressed the animation control to show her walking. Her thighs led to the cleft between her legs, making her body appear as if she were an exotic dancer.

Guido was in agony with his hardness when the operator switched off the screen to show David Schilling. Guido felt himself getting back in control of his reflexes.

The image of David Schilling in his khakis showed him walking and displayed his muscular body. *No matter,* thought Guido, *I can take him out in seconds.*

Then the full size figure of Ruth Reilly, a mirror image of her mother, Nancy, revealed a tall sensuous blond with blue eyes and very ample breasts. She had a bock pack strapped to her back as she walked through the college campus. The scene showed men stopping to look at her as she walked by. This was a woman of classic beauty. Guido could picture how she would perform to perfection in the art of sex.

He was erect again and almost overwhelmed with desire. "Guido, do you understand the importance of these two young women?" asked the Bishop impatiently. He had observed Guido's excitement, but *never mind; rewards must follow important works for the Church. All the more confidence that Guido will do what is necessary.*

Guido came back to reality, "Yes your eminence all I need is help in planning the apprehensions."

"We first must get a message to Nancy Reilly that she should stop her research about the lost books of the Bible and her fact finding trips to Europe. She is currently planning a trip to the Vatican to visit Monsignor Dominick Averti. That must never happen. She will be threatened with the life of her daughter."

"David Schilling has been warned but he is a very stubborn man. With the writings that you took from his computer, we know the danger with him is that in his accomplishments as a writer he could spread lies about the lost books, Mary Magdalene, Jesus Christ, and do great harm to the works of the Church. His skills could cause wide spread circulation of his book by a publisher, perhaps even as a best seller. His talents in presenting the history and the written word, takes the form of a very readable novel, one that could be featured in every book store. Others may have done more research and may have more information, but their writings are clinical-professorial and not generally palatable to the consumer public,"

Guido was getting his confidence back. He knew he could take out the women, have his fun, make their deaths appear accidental, and have no risk of discovery of his sexual impositions. His fantasy went as far as picturing them both in bondage, at the same time, with him as the master.

His first mission was right here in Washington, just a tune up with David Schilling. He knew exactly where to find him. Then he would get down to the fun part with Ruth Reilly before his trip to Germany for Maria Albrecht.

CHAPTER 27

▼

DAVID SCHILLING, HIS OTHER SIDE. WASHINGTON D.C. 2005

David left Nancy's office at the library and was feeling rather stressed and depressed. He wondered if he was becoming infatuated with Nancy. He found himself thinking about her and contacting her consistently. He had told himself that this was a professional interest and that they could collaborate in their research to benefit his writing. Now he was not so sure. Nancy had to decline his dinner invitation because of previous commitments at the library and a meeting with her daughter.

His son, in Ohio, informed him today that he was concerned about his marriage but David's grandchildren, a girl and a boy, were fine. He hadn't seen them for weeks and was remorseful about that. He had tried all day to reach his daughter by phone without success.

Damn, it seems as if I am always all alone to deal with my frustrations. His faith and his spiritual life were secure but sometimes he just wanted to lash out in anger at something. The homeless man on the street corner was sitting on the sidewalk leaning with his back to the building, his withered legs under him. "Hey, buddy, help a veteran. I just need a hot meal."

David looked down at him and thought, *yeah, sure, you don't want a hot meal, you want a drink—to get drunk. Okay, I can understand that. So do I. What in Hell is wrong with our society, here is this man just blocks from the Nation's capitol, the richest, most powerful country in the world, and we can't take care of our poor? Maybe this is a true test of the freedoms in our country. He has the right to be here and not to be carted off to jail or to some institution.*

David took out his money clip and handed two fifty dollar bills to the man. "God Bless you buddy, God Bless you." David walked away thinking, *at least this is one positive thing I have done today.*

He was not paying attention to where he was walking and when he looked up from his disjointed thoughts, he was in front of the Prime Rib restaurant. Without hesitating he entered the front door and went right to the bar.

"A dry Absolute martini, up, with olive," said David to the smiling bar tender. The bar was crowded with the after work crowd. He finished the martini quickly and ordered another while thinking to himself, *I know this is trouble to be drinking these things straight up. I'll stop at two.* After the third martini he was feeling bold and aggressive. Shaken loose from his reverie he looked around the bar to see two very attractive women sitting across from him. They smiled. He smiled back. The next thing he knew he was standing behind them making small talk. They both were well dressed and very engaging.

Looking at his Khaki outfit, "Did you just come off a safari?" said the one with sandy blond hair. She was about forty five, well built and seemed to be available. She was wearing an expensive, tailored, business suit.

"Yes I did, and I am about ready to go back," David said, slurring his words slightly.

"Oh where are you going?" Her name was Monica. She leaned into David and purred.

"To Germany and then to Italy. Would you like to go with me?" He was feeling very confident, now, and was about to make a conquest.

"Sure, when do we leave?" Monica said smiling.

The banter continued for a while; then Monica's friend excused her self to leave for an appointment. David took her empty seat. "What do you do here in Washington?" asked David. He was beginning to recover control of his speech.

"I work for a political consulting company."

"Oh that means that you are putting me on about traveling. You couldn't get away could you?"

"Not necessarily. I have some time built up for vacation and travel." She leaned even closer to David and said, "You smell good. What kind of cologne are you wearing?"

Monica lit a cigarette and David ordered drinks for both of them. She reached under the bar for his hand and squeezed it.

"Don't you have a husband or a boyfriend?" David was getting excited and was in a no caution zone because of the number of martinis.

"Not right now," Monica said, squeezing his hand even tighter.

He could feel the heat rising between them.

"Where are you staying David?"

"The Ritz-Carlton on K Street. They have a really nice dining room there. Would you like to join me for dinner?"

She looked at him and smiled. "Maybe I can. Let me make a call first." She dialed a number on a cell phone and turned away from the bar for a short conversation. "That sounds nice," she said after hanging up.

They took a taxi to the hotel. As they passed the elevator in the lobby, David said, "I need to go to my room and freshen up. Do you need to use the facilities?"

Once inside the room Monica walked to the window to look out over the terrace at the street scene. David walked up behind her. She turned and David embraced her. They were in bed making love before any more conversation.

Later, after a short nap, they were cuddled in the luxury of satin sheets and the cozy down comforter. "My God that was wonderful," David said, starting to sober up. We never did eat. Would you like to order room service?"

She looked at him with a sparkling smile, "Maybe you didn't eat but I did."

With that David felt his excitement return and they made love again.

Finally, at one o'clock in the morning Monica said, "David I hate to go. This has been so nice, but I have to get up early for work in the morning. Can I see you again before you leave town?"

"I was just about to ask you that. I have to go back to Ohio on Saturday to attend to family business. What are you doing tomorrow night?"

They made a date to meet at the Prime Rib at six o'clock the following afternoon. David spent all day driving to various locations in the D.C. area to gather data for his research. The thought of Monica and the evening they spent together occupied the back of his mind. His anticipation of seeing her tonight erased all thoughts about Nancy Reilly.

At four o'clock he arrived at his hotel for a short nap and a shave and shower before going to meet Monica. The message light was blinking on his phone but he was too tired to check it.

He arrived at the Prime Rib about ten minutes early, took a seat at the bar, and ordered a drink. *No martinis today. They almost wiped me out last night.*

At ten minutes after six, David looked at his watch again. *This is typical of women, to be fashionably late.* At six thirty, still no Monica, David asked the bartender to hold his seat while he looked around the dining room's waiting area.

At six forty-five he said to the bartender, "Excuse me but I was in here last night talking with two women. Do you happen to remember them?"

"Oh sure, you mean Monica, the one that you left with."

"You noticed, huh?" David said with a sheepish grin.

"Ah well, that is part of a bartender's job."

"She was supposed to meet me here at six o'clock and I don't know where to call her."

"She comes in here once in a while," said the bartender. "She leaves with different guys from time to time."

David frowned, "She told me she works for a political consulting firm."

With a knowing smile, the bartender said, "We have a lot of 'Political Consultants' in Washington. You know, with all the out of town politicians here without their wives and girl friends."

Aghast, David said, "You mean?"

"She is probably a high class call girl."

"A hooker! Oh my God!"

David ordered a martini and another one while he thought over last night. He knew it was too good to be true. Why hadn't she charged him or mentioned money to him?

Fighting a hang-over from last night and with a couple of martinis under his belt, he was feeling lonely and pissed off. He crossed the street on the way to his hotel and there was a nudie bar, with all the inviting signs and flashing lights. *What the Hell lets go in and see some of those big titted girls.*

They ushered him to a crowded bar on the upper level. A girl in her early twenties was making love to the brass pole with her legs entwined around it and her bare breasts bobbing up and down invitingly. David had two martinis and got up to stuff dollar bills in the dancers' stocking. As he sat back down, the guy behind him said, "Hey old man, sit down I can't see."

David turned around and said, "How would you like to go fuck yourself you God Dammed punk!"

The man said, "Hey asshole."

David turned and grabbed him, punched him and threw him to the floor. The bouncers were there immediately, and had to restrain David. They took him out of the room and held him until the police took him away in hand cuffs.

He was sitting in the station with his hands cuffed behind his back. Starting to sober up he said, "Officer what is happening here?"

The officer, a friendly type, and not one of the arresting policemen that hauled David into the station, looked up from his computer and said, "I am just finishing the background information on you. It doesn't look like you have ever been in trouble before. What happened?"

David said, "I really have no excuse other than I have had some rough times lately and just had too much to drink. Do you think I need a lawyer?"

"I don't think so. All we have here is drunk and disorderly and resisting arrest. There is no previous record on you, and the profile information indicates that you have been a reputable business person. It says here that you are from Ohio. What are you doing in Washington?"

"I am doing research for a book that I am writing. I retired from my real estate business several years ago. I am leaving town in two days to go home. Isn't there anything I can do to get released?"

"Let me go talk to the sergeant at the desk with the information we have on you."

David looked around the room. The handcuffs were biting into his wrists and his shoulders were hurting from the unnatural position. *I sure as Hell can't be any threat to anyone in this position. What a dumb shit you are David.* He couldn't even sit back properly with his hands behind his back. All he could do was kind of squat on the front of the chair. *Martinis and women have always caused me a boat load of trouble. When will you ever learn?*

The officer came back, sat down and said, "Well Mr. Schilling this is your lucky day. We called the night club and the owner didn't want to press charges. So all you have to do is pay a bond and you can be released."

"Oh, a bond. How much is that? Will there be anything on my record?"

"There will be nothing on the record. All you have to do is go back to your hotel and sleep it off. The bond is two hundred dollars."

David awakened the next morning with a splitting head ache, but grateful for his narrow escape. His short fuse temper, something that had caused him trouble before, was something he was going to have to work on.

After a pot of coffee and breakfast from room service he listened to his phone message: "David, this is Monica. I am really sorry. I can not meet you tonight. I had an emergency with the business. Please don't be angry with me. I enjoyed being with you so much! I'll call you so we can get together the next time you are in Washington."

This is just another mysterious event in my crazy world. I need to get back to Ohio for a while and get myself grounded.

CHAPTER 28

▼

DAVID AT HOME IN OHIO
2005

The short flight to Columbus gave David time to disconnect from his recent happenings and to begin the re-orientation process with his home and family. It was a beautiful sunny day. From the airplane window, the farm fields looked neat and orderly, arranged precisely on their North—South and East—West section lines. In the hilly areas, the farming patterns were less orderly and more interesting with corn rows, wheat and hay fields winding around the slopes in pin-wheel fashion. Much of this area is influenced by the Amish and the Mennonites. He thought back over the last few years, and contrasted his traveling about the globe, with the place-bound Amish farmers having no telephones, electricity, cars or the internet. His own childhood beginnings were on the farm, though abundant with backward customs; there was a learning environment with preparation for the technology of the future. Somewhere in the broad scope of his social structure was the ideal place for him. He wasn't exactly sure where.

As his son drove him back to the New England style village just East of Columbus, he could feel his world change, just like viewing a new page from the internet on his computer screen. Entrepreneurs had traveled to Ohio, bought this land, designed the town, and then sold shares to their neighbors in Granville

Massachusetts. This all happened around 1800 and the results were a picture post card New England village with a strong Welsh influence.

The Episcopal Church, a beauty in its Greek Revival architecture, was crowned by a shiny gold leaf dome. Tourists and local people were sitting at the sidewalk cafes. David thought of "Walden Pond", and reflected, *I need to take time to travel right here at home some day.*

His driveway was about a quarter mile long, winding and lined with trees. At the end was his Mediterranean style home, a design that was influenced by a trip to Spain many years ago. This was a sharp contrast to the Colonial styles of the village. His black Mercedes Benz, a compromise to buying American, was waiting in the garage, as was the tennis court in his back yard. *I wonder if I can get the tennis gang together on short notice.*

He thought back over the two marriages he had experienced here, the raising of his son and daughter, and the various social events, including marriages, held in the spacious court yard. He expelled a deep sigh at the end of this kaleidoscope. His son said, "Dad, what is wrong? What were you thinking about?"

"Oh, just all the 'water that has flowed over the dam' in the past thirty years. Thanks for picking me up at the airport. It really feels good to be home."

He walked through the garage into the laundry room, the kitchen, and the long gallery serving as a hallway. He stopped to look at the photo portraits of family, sturdy Germanic stock, dating back seven generations, to the 1830's. Some of his oil paintings and sketches from as far back as forty years ago and various other family artifacts brought back fleeting memories. This was the beginning of getting "grounded."

At the end of the hall he entered his bedroom, dropped the bags and changed into a pair of tennis shoes. A walk down the bike path, adjoining his back yard, allowed further settling and a firming up of the distant wall to the world he had just left. A stream followed the path, once a railroad, and led past the cemetery where he would finally rest, then through the, still functioning, grain mill and on into the village.

This wasn't going to be a long walk, just a get-acquainted one. So many things have changed here in the past thirty years, things that a casual visitor would miss. The landmark opera house had burned down years ago. Nineteen over-eager policemen replace the lone Red Petit, the constable reigning when I arrived. The Rexall drug store has moved to a new location. The wide boulevard is naked without the center street parking it used to have. There are bars, now, in defiance of the long term ban of alcohol from the Baptist beginnings. The farmers that walked the streets are gone in favor of young urban professionals and their BMWs and Volvos. Most of the brick paving has been covered by blacktop. The Denison University students are gone for the summer, leaving a deficit of speeding tickets and tailgaters.

There is a "Gotcha" philosophy from the newly crowned politicians on city council. The liberals at the Chamber of Commerce are trying to find ways to stop business. God forbid if you want to change the paint color of your house. Don't ever mention the fact that the town is a planned development community created by profit seeking settlers. The liberal faction from "the hill" [the University professors and their friends] still protest everything at every gathering. In spite of all the self-appointments to the deity of village government, it is still a neat place to be. If only the yuppies would stop passing school tax levies and driving all the old folks out of town. They should be required to sign a contract to stay and pay the taxes after their kids are graduated, instead of moving to a sunny condominium location.

As I pass the Inn, a replicated English Manor House, I think about the woman that inherited it and then lost it because of financial difficulties. She was a big woman, colorful, controversial, and unforgettable. She and her sister, each, inherited a fortune from their father. Her sister invested well and was very financially secure. The woman's interest in theatre led her to investments in Broadway plays, local tent theatre productions with professional actors, and a generally passionate obsession with entertainers. These diversions, along with poor management of her money and her farm, caused her to lose everything, including the Inn, to foreclosure. She had been married once, but later was said to favor relationships with other women. Regardless of her divergent behavior, her absence to the village left a void of entertainment and speculation.

Instead of stopping at this "watering hole" I decided to finish my walk home. In my home office, I took the laptop from its case, and inserted it into the docking port of the computer system. While waiting for the systems check from the internet and the hard drive, I looked around the room at the warm and waiting books, files, maps and other reference materials that were tools of my quest for expression. My thoughts ranged far back over the events of my travels and the history of all the violence in the events leading to our present world and its religions, customs, languages, social structures and wars. Then I thought about this peace of this little village, its people, and the relative likeness to other villages.

It felt good to be here in this sanctuary from the outside world. The symphonic music from his stereo system helped calm me. Since my first encounter with a symphony orchestra, at Radio City Music Hall, in New York, I have been hooked on classical music. I was eighteen, at the time, on a trip with the high school graduating seniors. Everyone was horsing around, not paying attention to this boring place, when the lights focused on the orchestra rising from the pit. I was hypnotized, breathless, changed for life.

How should I approach the rest of my research and the compelling need to leave my opinions in the form of a book? *I will just put these thoughts aside for a while and enjoy the moment.*

———

Guido left the Ritz-Carlton Hotel in Washington, disappointed that David had checked out. His computer had been able to access the Hotel's records and when he saw that David was gone, he decided to check the desk in person. He had no idea where David was going next, but he could find out, quickly, and finish him. He had never been to Ohio. All he had to do was to get the Bishop's permission.

CHAPTER 29

▼

DOMINICK AVERTI— ROME 1978

Dominick stayed near the walls and crept through alleys on his way back to the Vatican. His fear was overpowering. He couldn't imagine that after all his years of dedication to the Church and the exercise of good judgment, often missing in young persons, that he had done such a stupid thing. Now, how can he ever counsel others about sin? The woman had appeared in his life almost like a divine apparition.

He hadn't eaten for hours but there was no hunger for anything other than safety and the restoration of his station at the Vatican. They would be waiting to question his absence and to banish him from the Order forever. What would he do with the rest of his life?

The Vatican was heavily secured by the Swiss Guard. This was not like sneaking into a building but was intrusion into a sovereign country. What was he to do; walk right up to the entrance gate; look for a service entrance through the walls? He stood at a corner looking across the street at the gate. Of course tourists entered here several times a day. Could he pose as one of them? No, he would most certainly be recognized by the guards. He had thoughts about running away but where would he go?

There was obviously an alert and a search for him after the discovery that the Pope's quarters had been abandoned. While Dominick was concerned, his natural aggressiveness, just like on the soccer field, prevailed. He decided to go directly to the gate and enter while the guard was busy checking a service vehicle. He was almost past the gate, and safely inside, when a dog in the vehicle began growling and barking fiercely at him. Instead of drawing attention to him, the driver and the guard, were startled by the dog's sudden outburst. They missed seeing Dominick, completely.

Now he was inside the walls; what next? He couldn't get inside the Pope's area without his clerical uniform.

The laundry area was behind a group of buildings off to his right. There were hedges to walk near so that he was not in plain sight. He rounded the corner and as luck would have it a door that should have been secured was standing open. He looked both ways on the narrow street and seeing no one, approached the door, and carefully looked inside. He could hear voices and equipment running. As he crept down the hallway and turned the corner, there stood a rolling coat rack with freshly cleaned clerical uniforms. He deftly grabbed one, went inside a rest room, and closed and locked the door.

He was sweating profusely from the anxiety. The uniform fit well enough. He fashioned a clerical collar from a paper towel that would pass without close inspection. There were several obstacles to pass and persons to greet before he could get to the Pope's quarters. How, then, would he get inside once he arrived there? The network of corridors, stairways, and elevators were known to few, as well as Dominick knew them. He opened a seldom used stairway door and there in front of him was the entrance to the Pope's quarters with an armed guard sitting at the desk.

He could not believe his good fortune; the guard was Julius, one of the few friendly members of the Swiss Guard staff. Dominick swallowed, took a deep breath, and walked up to the guard. The guard had been concentrating on the surveillance cameras and didn't notice Dominick until he stood right in front of him. Dominick had avoided the view range of the cameras. Julius looked up, startled, and said, "Dominick, where have you been?"

Dominick made a half smile and said, "What do you mean?"

"Listen," said Julius, "I know you were gone. I have been covering for you for hours. Where have you been?"

"I had to leave momentarily and then found I was locked out. I panicked and spent the night in the laundry area," he lied.

"Well this is your lucky day Dominick. I have to get you safely back inside in order to prevent trouble for both of us."

Inside the Pope's quarters Dominick saw that the bookcase door to the secret tunnel entrance was still open. He closed it and fell to his knees in prayer. "Dear Lord I beg your forgiveness. I have sinned. You must have great works for me to have allowed a second chance."

He gave vows to himself to re-dedicate his life to research, learning about the Vatican archives, and the search for answers to the many questions that were surfacing as he gathered more and more information. There were areas in the archives that he had not yet been privileged to visit but his teachers assured him that his time would come. The preservation of priceless and fragile documents, that were known to be one of a kind in the Vatican, was his primary training. Only a few persons in the world would have access. Since the Vatican was built upon the foundations of other ancient buildings, churches, crypts, and secret tunnels, the technical aspects of climate control, moisture, light infiltration, rodents, and security were challenges in addition to the actual cataloging and understanding of the vast library of information. No one individual in the Vatican was entrusted with complete control.

Some of the documents, books and information were of such controversial nature, including questionable authors and sources, that their release to the world could create chaos to the church and to mankind. The security issues of thievery ranged from the fear of document destruction to the world market for authenticated material. The lost books of the Bible, for example, were said to be held in protection by the Vatican, never to be released. The Protestant perception of the Catholic Church banning books and information to its parishioners had some validity based on fact. Certain members of the Church, such as Bishop Rhein in Germany, fought for enlightenment, much to their detriment.

Dominick was a believer but sometimes struggled with the Catholic doctrine that only members of the clergy had direct access to God. Why weren't all the followers privileged to have their own private meditation with God? It seemed that his progress in the archives was being very carefully controlled as if trust and information were being doled out in direct proportion to his advances in age. As a child, Bishop Rhein, in the German Alpine village, had encouraged him to think somewhat outside the norm for Catholic teaching. Dominick had been sent there for six months of training because of the Bishop's expertise in ancient documents.

Feeling safe inside the Pope's quarters, he checked the bookcase where it had led to the tunnel, and could not detect the opening at all. He was looking around the area to see what he might have pressed to cause the door to swing open. The shrill ring of the phone startled him. "Dominick, this is Carmerlengo Campesi. Is everything intact there? The Pope is returning tomorrow."

Dominick hesitated, looked around the room, and stuttered slightly, "Ya, Yes your eminence. Everything is fine."

"Come to my office immediately. I want to talk with you about the last forty eight hours you have spent there."

"Certainly sir, but who will guard the Pope's quarters?" He was feeling very anxious about the questioning.

"I have arranged for the Swiss Guard to take over," said the Carmerlengo, impatiently.

CHAPTER 30

▼

NANCY, FLIGHT TO PARIS—GUIDO, 2005

Nancy looked out the window of the 747 at the Potomac River and the diminishing scene below her. *Everything looks so orderly down there,* she thought. Out over the ocean, she dropped her seat back, relaxed and thought back over the frenzied week of preparation for the trip. *In a city, no, a world, known for chaos, it is comforting to get above it all to look at the bigger perspective. Maybe that is how God sees it.* The plethora of problems she had encountered seemed distant, now, and not real. Her daughter, Ruth, was safe with her father in the Catskills after the chilling anonymous phone call warning her not to go to Europe or her daughter was in danger.

The chardonnay she was sipping allowed her to release the tension in her neck and shoulders. She closed her eyes for a second and woke up three hours later to find her head against the window and her cheek wet from the saliva that ran from the relaxed state of her mouth. Self conscious, she straightened in her seat, wiped her cheek and looked around. No one was watching. The nap was just the ticket she needed to think about the trip ahead of her. She took the itinerary from her handbag and studied it. She couldn't help envisioning herself at a sidewalk café in Paris sipping wine with a stranger, in pleasant conversation, on a bright sunny day. *Wait a minute, Nancy,* she said to herself. *You are going to have time for nothing but business on this trip.*

Hot flashes were making Nancy very uncomfortable. She was afraid that she was going to have her period in the midst of all this travel. The airplane made a steep bank while approaching the airport in Paris. She had pain medication in her purse but was reluctant to take it until absolutely necessary.

I wish men had to experience menopause. Forty nine; isn't that too young for me to be suffering this? With periods now coming every three or four months how in the Hell can I plan anything? There is no explaining how I feel or nothing that can please me when this happens.

She took deep breaths and tried to calm herself. She was squirming in her seat so much that the man next to her turned and looked her way. "Miss, are you all right?" he said.

She smiled and said, "Oh sorry it has just been a busy trip and I am feeling slightly nauseous."

She was at the window and he was seated at the aisle. "Do you need to get out and walk around?" he said.

"Thank you, but I think I'll be fine. Maybe when the plane levels out I will."

"Just let me know," he said.

———

Guido, thwarted from finding Nancy's daughter, Ruth, and David Schilling, had a sudden change of plans, after consultation with the Bishop. He had a copy of Nancy's exact itinerary and was on his way to find Maria Albrecht in Germany and then to catch up with Nancy in Rome. His operative counter part in Paris was following Nancy and would report her activities to the Bishop. Their world wide satellite net work made the reporting of information very easy. He could literally "kill two birds with one stone", by finding David Schilling and Nancy Reilly when they came together in Rome. He would have already had his fun with Maria by that time.

CHAPTER 31

▼

MARIA'S SEARCH FOR INFORMATION

Haunted by the memories of her experiences at the Castle Inn, the village monastery, the mysterious phone call to her mother, and then the visit from Lotar Herron, Maria was racing down the Autobahn from Berlin to her childhood home in the Alps.

"Maria, where are you?" Rolfe shouted into the mobile phone.

After getting back into cellular range she checked her messages. "Oh the Hell with this and the Hell with him!" He was starting to suffocate her. Why did this always happen to her with men that she was attracted to?

She erased all the messages and turned off the phone.

The beautifully engineered highways took some of the fun out of the driving in her Mercedes Benz sports car. She remembered the hair pin curves in the old roads and the thrill of speeding around them.

"Mother, can you go with me to the monastery? I have to satisfy my curiosity about what happened to Bishop Rhein."

"Maria some things are better left alone."

"How can you say that, Mother? You have always encouraged me to be independent and to pursue my interests. I need to get this mystery settled in my mind so I can concentrate on my career."

"What do you want out of life, child?" She knew better than to question Maria directly about the conflict with her career and marriage and family.

"Mother, I honestly don't know. I have these visions of settling down with a nice home and family, but the theatre keeps tugging at me. Every time I meet some one and start to think seriously about marriage and children, a new opportunity opens up that I feel compelled to go after. Then it seems that I always pick the wrong man or he picks me. Am I doomed to make that same mistake time after time? My analyst says that a majority of women have a pattern of relationships with men that are not right for them."

Her mother wisely just looked at Maria and did not answer.

"I have begun to make so much money, that I could probably leave the theatre and retire on what I already have. But money just doesn't seem to be the answer."

"Darling, no one can answer that question for you. If you pray for answers, and let go, the solutions should come to you."

Maria looked down at the coffee cup and realized how tightly she was gripping it in her anxiety. "I wish I could talk with Bishop Rhein again. He always made me feel wise and helped me think for myself. He was like a father or a grandfather to me. His disappearance, Mother; do you think he was kidnapped or that he just went away to go into hiding?"

Angelina got up from her chair, and walked to the window, to look outside. She turned and looked back at a perplexed, Maria. She went back to Maria, brushed a lock of hair back from her forehead and said, "You might want to talk with Lotar Herron at the Castle Inn at Etal. I don't know if he is there now or if he is on theatrical tour."

"Why would I want to talk with him, Mother? He tried to approach me at a private party in my dressing room on my birthday. I have no idea how he got into the room. Rolfe stopped him and sent him away. I haven't heard about him since then."

"He is a strange, but very powerful person, Maria, and he knew Bishop Rhein well."

"I wish I had known my father and more about him." Maria looked dejectedly at her mother.

Angelina did not make eye contact. She turned and started walking towards the kitchen. "Maria, I have told you all there is to tell about him, up until the time of his disappearance. You had only just turned two."

CHAPTER 32

▼

NANCY IN PARIS, DEPARTURE FOR ROME

I was met at Charles DeGaulle airport by a guide, holding a sign with my name. He met me just outside the gate, where the customs agent didn't even give me a nod of recognition. It was a 45 minute ride to the Hotel Soffitel Le Parc on Rue Raymond Poincare'.

The hotel staff was exceptionally friendly and helpful upon my arrival, starting with the doorman, the desk clerk, the concierge, and a staff coordinator. It was a small but elegant reception area with a library off to the side and a bar behind the front desk. I was taken to my room by a friendly young woman. The hotel entrance is modest but when we walked out of the lobby and through the passageway, built for horse and carriage access, a large courtyard area was revealed with tables, fountains and sculptures, surrounded by the multiple floor hotel, meeting rooms and dining room.

I acquainted myself with the room while my bag was being delivered. I tipped the smiling bellman and then spent a few minutes freshening up in the bathroom. Even though I was tired, the lure of Paris drew me to study my map and begin acquaintance with the city by taking a walk.

I went to Victor Hugo Circle and then the Avenue Victor Hugo, towards the Arc de Triumphe. The streets were spotlessly clean. My excitement began to build as would any woman's, when I passed one designer shop after another. I was determined, however, to keep my focus on the City and not allow this to develop into a shopping trip.

I arrived at the Arc de Triumphe in less than fifteen minutes, surprised at how close were the landmarks that I had seen in the media since childhood. The Eiffel Tower, was imposing, only blocks away. What is so different here? I thought. Then it occurred to me that the major attractions were out in the open, and not hidden by surrounding tall buildings. My guide had told me that Napoleon had demolished much of the center of Paris to create wider streets and open vistas. It certainly worked. It was wonderful to have such a pedestrian friendly ambiance. In spite of the controversy he created with the demolition and the loss of historic edifice, Napoleon's genius for looking to the future made the streets an attraction for the enjoyment of people on foot. The result was self contained neighborhoods, each blending into another. Restaurants, small stores, shops, apartments, and businesses in a compatible format of co-existence display the old world concept of neighborhood, to which we are just now re-discovering in the United States. The passing of the "Big Box" shopping center, miles away from residences, is a trend and a welcome demise.

I stood looking at the controversial glass pyramid at the entrance to the Louvre. "Madame would you like a guided tour of the Louvre," a seedy looking man, small, dark, and needing a shave, moved to within a few inches of me. He smelled of stale alcohol and tobacco.

I stepped away from him, smiled and said, "No, thank you."

"But mademoiselle I can save you money and show you secret places," he persisted, following her.

I clutched my purse tightly and continued to walk away. The man followed me until a gendarme appeared at the corner. I walked toward the policeman. The man stopped and walked the other way.

I have been warned about pickpockets and muggers. Maybe I should wait for my guide tomorrow before venturing further, today. Oh, but my time here is so limited.

Henri LeFarve, one of the senior curators at the Louvre, was not available until tomorrow morning. Her main objective, here, to view the Mona Lisa, was part of her discovery plan for Leonardo DaVinci's works that would be completed in Italy. Her document research at the Vatican, and her appointment to see "The Last Supper" in Milan, caused her schedule to have little free time.

I would not know when my meeting with David Schilling in Rome was going to take place until I checked into my hotel near the Vatican. Special access to many limited viewing artifacts was being presented to me on this trip because of my status at the Washington D.C. library and my acquaintance with Dominick Averti.

So many conflicts with the teachings of my early Protestant background had my head virtually spinning with questions. What is the real story about Mary Magdalene? The life of Jesus Christ had so many different interpretations. How much did Leonardo DaVinci really know about the Last Supper and the Disciples? After all, his works were fifteen hundred years later. Old Testament issues dating back to King Solomon thousands of years before Christ were rampant with questions about the Jewish faith, the original Masonic order, the Knights Templar, and many of the religious symbols in use today, including the cross. In spite of the many libraries, art works, temples, building structures, customs and general prejudices, how does all this conflict affect the spiritual philosophy of man?

I was wondering if I was in danger of learning too much, so much that would shake the foundations of my spirituality and endanger the serenity that I could gather when all Hell was breaking loose in my life. I knew there was a possibility that I was being stalked by evil forces. I was concerned about my daughter, Ruth, but in actuality not fearful about my own life.

I realized that I was just standing still. I shook off the trance, took a final look at the Louvre, then turned and walked back to my hotel. The impact of the huge paved area at the Louvre, and the contrast between the modern glass pyramid at the entrance with the baroque architecture from the King's palaces and the adjoining buildings, that had played a dramatic part in French history, left me with many more questions.

I had a light supper at the hotel and decided to go to bed early so that I would be rested for the trip and fresh for the busy schedule in Paris. Because of my fears about telephone privacy, I could not call Ruth in the Catskills.

Before going to sleep I looked out over the lights of Paris, and then thought back over my years of research and the surprise about the major influence of the French on the Reformation period and the influence on Christian history. *Why have the French always been out of step with the rest of the World? It seems that they can not be allies with any country. Or is that just a perception generated by the American Press and our government?* In addition to the Louvre, I would visit two small rare book dealers while in Paris. Exhausted, I fell asleep quickly.

————

The viewing of Da Vinci's Mona Lisa had been a little disappointing. The painting was very small and not as imposing as all the commercial characterizations. A group of Asian teenagers was busy snapping hundreds of flash photos in an area where flash cameras were forbidden. The curator and I both expressed our displeasure over that, but the guards just stood by without comment. I was over whelmed by the volume of art and wished I had a week or two in Paris instead of three days. The history behind the buildings at the Louvre was a study in itself that would take days. *Some day I will return.*

The curator, Henri LeFarve, was wonderful with his knowledge and charm. He was certainly an opposite of the negative impression that most Americans held about the French. We spent almost four hours moving from one section of the Louvre to the next. The object was to acquaint me with the general layout and to make me feel comfortable with the map of the four floors that stretched out over three city blocks. The sculptures of Winged Victory and Aphrodite, known as Venus de Milo, were major attractions on separate floors, each, in a big assembly area in a stairway.

Napoleon III's apartment was a study in the excesses demanded and enjoyed by monarchs. His ego, was not fueled by the military successes that his ancestor, Napoleon Bonaparte', had achieved. His lack of accomplishment and his quest for power was assuaged by the self indulgent display of gold and glitter. He did not leave a generally favorable legacy.

There was a nice shopping area and various food courts accessible by escalators off the reception area under the glass pyramid. A serious art historian could spend weeks, here, or return for short visits over a lifetime. After my guide left, I spent two more hours, after lunch, wandering around exhibits of special interest to me. After studying the Rubens and Van Dyke paintings on the top floor at the "Richelieu" wing, I was exhausted, with my brain on art overload.

I had an early dinner at Le Train Bleu, a large dining room, in an old palace gallery, attached to the railroad station. The food was excellent, but expensive, and the gold, glitter, chandeliers and frescoes all added to an uncommon and worthwhile spectacle. The train station, itself, kept my attention for several minutes. The high speed trains, under the glass canopy, accommodated travelers who took efficient train travel for granted. The contrast with the United State's limited and out dated rail system caused me to think bitterly about the oil and rubber companies that consciously helped destroy trains so that they could profiteer with their tires and gasoline.

After two glasses of wine in the hotel bar and following pleasant conversation with the bartenders, I was ready to rest, and make my plans for the next day. In my room, I studied maps and then called the concierge desk to make a reservation at the Musee d' Orsay for the next morning. I fell asleep with a book in my hand and one of the two English speaking television stations turned on.

———

It was a Sunday morning and I felt like a brisk walk past the Eiffel Tower and along the Seine River. After a few blocks I buttoned my overcoat up to the neck and congratulated myself for having the fore sight to bring warm clothing to Paris. Thank goodness for the weather forecasts from the Internet. France was having an unusual cold spell, with this morning temperature in the 20's Fahrenheit, and the wind gusting at about 15 knots, the wind-chill factor was from zero to five degrees.

My destination was the Musee d' Orsay through the University Area on the Left Bank. After a short time on the river walk where the tour boats with diners on board, passed, on their trip around the city, I gave in to the cold and moved over to Rue de l'Universite'. This was a long street shielded from the wind by buildings and passed only a block away from d' Orsay. After about 45 minutes, while building my resolve to take taxi cabs for these long hikes, I arrived, frozen, at the museum.

This was another former railroad station, elegant in its refurbished museum format. My primary destination was the third floor French Impressionist Gallery. Since I had made plans to tour Paris in cold weather, I escaped major crowds of tourists, thus avoiding lines, and waiting, to see what I wanted to see. For this reason, I was unprepared for throngs of people in the Impressionist Gallery. I was somewhat out of sorts because I could not walk right up to a painting that I wanted to study.

I saw an opening in another room where the crowds had parted, so I walked quickly there, turned the corner, and stood face to face, only inches away from Vincent Van Gogh's "Self Portrait". Next to it was "Sunflowers." I was shocked; this was surreal almost as in a dream. These are paintings that I have admired for a lifetime. Why I was most interested in Van Gogh, in the midst of all the other Impressionists, I am not sure. His work is easy to recognize because his style is so distinct and his subjects are approachable, in contrast to all the ethereal imaginings of the Great Masters. Perhaps I could just fantasize that I could duplicate his work with the brilliant color and sweeping brush strokes with my own amateur painting. I found over the years that I simply lacked patience for trying to duplicate the great detail that I see in nature. Van Gogh and many of the other Impressionists create the feeling of the "presence of now", as if the artist had just walked away from the canvas to attend to another chore, and would be right back.

————

That evening I went to the Au Pied De Cochon Brasserie at Rue Coquilliere, recommended by a friend from home. The taxi picked me up in front of the hotel, drove along the Seine River, past the Louvre, the ornate bridges, and some of the other landmarks that I had visited. I was starting to feel at home in the City. The sun was just descending over the horizon with its waning hues reflecting off the river. Life was good.

The driver stopped on a narrow, one way, street, with traffic behind. I handed him a fifty Euro bill.

"I am sorry Mademoiselle, no cash that. You go to restaurant get change." I ran inside, and the maitre d' kindly changed the bill.

I ran to the taxi, paid him, turned and hurried back to the restaurant. He drove off to relieve the traffic backed up behind him

The maitre d' said something in French. Parlez-vous anglais Monsieur?" I asked.

"Yes, Mademoiselle, dinner for one?"

"Yes, I" before I finished the sentence I reached into the purse for my wallet. It was not there. I rummaged through my suit pockets, no wallet. I looked to the counter where I had put my purse down when I ran back to the taxi. I looked back in my purse again, with my frustration growing.

"Is something wrong, Mademoiselle?" asked the maitre d' with a look of concern.

"Yes, I believe I lost my wallet. It must be in the taxi. Please excuse me." I ran back outside on the chance that the taxi driver had returned with my wallet. I looked all around on the street and the planter area where I left the cab.

Defeated, I walked back inside the restaurant. "I am sorry, I have lost my wallet. It must be in the taxi."

The maitre d' said, "Where did you leave from? Perhaps we can find the taxi."

His English was limited. He called two places that answered to Le Parc before I mentioned Soffitel. "Ah" he said, "That makes a difference"

While he was calling my hotel I was thinking, *My God, here I am in a foreign city of eleven million people and my wallet is gone, with everything, my credit cards, my driver's license, everything. This can't be happening to me. What will I do? Please, please let him find the hotel so they can reach the taxi company.*

He was talking to my hotel and had identified me as a resident there. I was beginning to be hopeful. When he hung up the phone he said, "I am sorry, they have no way to trace the taxi company. It was just the first one available. They do not keep record of those calls.

I was crestfallen!

"Do you have money?" he asked.

"Yes, I have money." I carried cash in a secret zipper pocket in my suit.

"Do you wish to have dinner."

"Yes sir, but I would like to have a drink first."

"Of course, Mademoiselle". He ushered me to a seat in the bar area.

As luck would have it all this was in the middle of a shift change so the maitre d' was preparing to leave for the day. I had to explain my dilemma to the waiter and another maitre d'. They were extremely friendly and gracious.

I needed the impact of a scotch instead of wine. While I was finishing the second drink I was making a list of the things in my wallet and thinking of the hassle that would follow in the restoration of everything. Fortunately, my passport was in the hotel room and I had cash. I wasn't sure if I could pay the hotel bill without the credit card and leave the country on a flight without my driver's license. Tomorrow I would have to find the American Embassy to see if they could help.

The scotch was beginning to take effect, and the "to Hell with it" attitude was growing. I am going to enjoy my dinner, and some wine and deal with it tomorrow. The wine, the dinner, and the service were exceptional. The people I have met in Paris have been laying the foundation for my appreciation of their warm friendliness. Again, I was wondering about the typical American perception of the haughtiness of the French. I certainly haven't seen that. In fact, I was being charmed by the small town neighbor feeling.

After dinner, I took a taxi back to Le Parc Hotel and was greeted by the desk clerk, the concierge and the bar tender. All expressed concern about the tale of my lost wallet. I thanked them and went to my room. As I was entering the phone was ringing.

"Hello." I said, wondering who could be calling me here.

"Did you find your wallet?" It was my administrative assistant from the library in Washington D.C.

"Valerie, how did you know about that?"

"Nancy, I had a call from your bank. [*I was calculating while she talked—it was 8:30 in the evening here so it must be 2:30 in the afternoon there*] A man found your wallet in the back seat of a taxi and called the bank. Do you want me to cancel your credit cards?"

"This is unbelievable. Do you have his name and address?"

"Yes, do you have a pencil and paper handy?"

She gave me all the information. I thanked her profusely and hung up. After trying in vain to dial his number using the unfamiliar phone system, I went to the front desk. The very friendly young woman there, reached him, and handed me the phone.

In twenty minutes I walked out of the old world elevator with the open steel grating, the kind you see in old movies like, Casablanca, down the hallway and there he stood in the doorway to his room with my wallet in hand.

"Mr. Kinlock?"

"Yes, is this your wallet?"

"Yes, you will never know how grateful I am. How did you find this? Where are you from?"

"I am from Brooklyn, New York. My wife and I must have been in the taxi just after you. The wallet was lying on the seat. I thought it would be better for me to call your bank than to turn it over to the taxi driver."

He was young, perhaps about 35, and wearing a yarmulke.

"Mr. Kinlock you will never know how large of a favor you have done for me. I was in panic."

He smiled and handed me the wallet.

"Please, I must reward you with the cash in here." There were about 250 Euro, a pittance compared with the relief I felt and the realization of saving all the days ahead getting my various identifications restored.

"Oh, no, no, I am happy I could help."

"But I insist. You don't know the favor you did for me."

"I sure you would have done the same for me or anyone else."

"Thank you, thank you. You have restored my faith in mankind."

I left the hotel where my taxi was still waiting. How lucky could I be? I really didn't expect the driver to still be there even though he promised. No one will believe this entire story.

———

The two rare book stores were well secured, and essentially disguised in an array of Antique shops near the Vatican. They were only blocks apart and would not be noticed by the casual tourist, without a guide. The first store was up a flight of steps and at the rear of a long hallway. Nancy rang the doorbell. A man came to the iron gate, securing the entryway, and spoke with her over the intercom. She announced her name and showed her credentials over the viewing camera.

The man was smallish and seemed very impatient. He took her to a section of documents and books dealing with the Bible, both current and the lost versions. He stood at her elbow, watching carefully, and responded to her questions with polite but terse answers. Nancy felt so hurried and uncomfortable that she thanked the man and left. She would certainly have to tell Dominick and her university correspondents that this was not a very friendly book store.

The other store was much more open and cheerful. At street level the interior was inviting and show cased by large windows. What Nancy did not see was the elaborate security system and the hidden security doors that would slam shut at the sound of an alarm.

"Yes Mademoiselle Reilly, we were expecting you. Please come in. May I offer you a cup of tea?" The big man bowed, smiled and ushered her to a small sitting room overlooking a walled in patio. "How was your flight and your hotel accommodation?"

"Thank you for asking, Mr. Verneau, I slept for almost the entire flight and the hotel is charming. I am very excited to be in Paris for my first visit to the Louvre and to your facility." Nancy sat back and relaxed while he poured her tea. This atmosphere certainly seemed different from the other book store she had visited.

"Have you spoken recently to our mutual friend, Monsignor Averti?"

"Yes, just before I left Washington. He had planned to meet me here, in Paris, but he encountered some issues at the Vatican, that has made his trip impossible."

"Oh that is too bad. I was looking forward to seeing him again. We have so much in common with our interests in ancient documents."

Nancy sat her cup on the small table, and said, "He asked me to give you his regards and his regrets. He said you were much more qualified than he to help with my research."

"Well I will certainly try." He smiled and said, "You and I have such mutual interests. The exchange of information from your library in Washington is invaluable to me."

Guido's operative was sitting across the street partly hidden by a tree. The operative had followed Nancy this morning. The instructions were to do nothing but to report her activities and the persons she came in contact with. Any information including possible changes in her schedule, would be forwarded so that

Guido could coordinate his trip to Germany, take care of his business with Maria Albrecht, and then go to Rome to dispatch Nancy and David Schilling.

"Mr. Verneau I am curious about the various references to the Knights Templar that I see in many places in your store."

They were walking down a circular stair two levels below the street.

He stopped, in surprise, and looked back to her. "You are certainly aware of the common ownership and the communications between here and your library in Washington, D.C."

"I am not sure what you mean." Nancy was uncomfortable in stopping on the stair where the lighting was poor.

"Let us continue to the vault and we can talk about this."

They reached a sealed door, opening into a large underground area. They had to pass through another sealed door while one closed behind them. "All of this is for security, lighting, and climate control so that the documents have the greatest chance of preservation." There were individual vaults around the center area of the room.

"Before we continue," said Verneau, "I am told that you are an Eastern Star. Is that correct?"

"Why yes," said Nancy, "how did you know?"

"Forgive me for answering a question with a question, but your father was also a Mason wasn't he?"

Nancy just stared at Verneau with out answering.

He smiled, "We have much more in common that you know. I did research about your background when I was informed of your visit."

Nancy, unable to hide her perplexity said, "I wish I had been informed of your interest in me. I could have given all that information directly."

"Please don't take offense Miss Reilly. We can work together. Come; let me show you documents about the Templar."

They went into a sealed vault, where the lighting was like the infra red in a photography developing room.

"The only other known copies of these documents are buried in the vaults at Rosslyn Chapel in Scotland. Even the Vatican does not have them."

"What does all this mean?" asked Nancy.

"This is simply documentation that the Knights Templar, after persecution by the Catholic Church in the early 1,300's, had to leave the Mediterranean area and flee to the North, finally settling in Scotland. They eventually helped drive the English troops out of Scotland and subsequently had a large influence upon the founding fathers, and the constitution of the United States."

"I have heard these theories," said Nancy after a hesitation. "There is a lot of controversy about all this."

"Indeed there is," said Verneau, "but we have documentation to give these theories credibility. Some organizations around the world would like to destroy this information. First, let me acknowledge to you that your library in Washington is dedicated to the preservation of the freedom of religion."

"Of course that is true," she said.

"The founding fathers of your country based the foundation of your government upon the principles of the Templar and the Masonic order."

"How do you know this?"

"Weren't Washington, Jefferson and Franklin members of the Masonic order?"

She just looked at him knowing the answer.

"Your library and this one is funded by an international organization dedicated to preserving freedoms. You are aware that the Knights Templar has enormous wealth from the banking systems developed in Europe during the Renaissance Period and that they still control that wealth today."

"Who are these people? Where do they operate from?" Nancy was getting frustrated.

"That is a question that can't be answered. It is rumored that the Templars have a secret organization inside a secret organization, comprised of only a handful of people in the world."

"Well, how could this organization be perpetuated?" she asked.

"Have you heard of the Priory of Scion?' he asked.

"Yes, but that is an ancient organization. They don't exist today, do they?"

"Again, I apologize for answering a question with a question. Is the Catholic Church still in existence and growing today?"

She just looked at him without answering.

He continued, "We are told that the Priory of Scion has been handed down through the centuries and that the members, only four or five, are hand picked by the survivors, upon the death of one. The power that they possess can not be revealed or compromised."

"Surely you don't believe that the Knights Templar or the Masons are behind all this do you?"

Now he didn't answer her directly. "Have you heard of the Opus Dei?"

"Of course; they even infiltrated our national security system." There was a moment of silence, then, she said, "Have you talked with Monsignor Averti about this?"

Verneau looked at her very intently. "I believe that you must be very careful what you reveal to the Monsignor. He may have directly opposing views to ours, and could place you in great danger."

"You can't be suggesting that my friend Monsignor Averti is an enemy of freedom just because he is a ranking person at the Vatican."

"Power is the basis of religion and government." Spirituality and faith are secondary."

"I don't believe that for a minute," said Nancy angrily. "Why is Rosslyn Chapel so important?"

"It was built by Sir William Saint Clair in 1447, the eleventh Baron of Roslyn and the third and last Earl of Orkney. The structure depicts world history in its appointments including items commonly thought of in the Masonic ritual today. His family was granted the position of Grand Master of the Order of Freemasonry of Scotland."

"Mr. Verneau, why are you telling me all this? I thought we were simply going to look at documents."

"Miss Reilly, our visit is much more important than looking at documents. How were you treated at the other book store before you came here?"

Nancy knew this was a loaded question. "Not very well, in fact rather rudely, why?"

"Those people are aligned with the Opus Dei and dedicated to suppression of the truth about the Bible, Jesus Christ and Mary Magdalene. You have been chosen, because of your background, to carry on with the search for truth and to help reveal the hidden light."

"What do you mean "hidden light"; I have been chosen by whom? This entire conversation is taking an uncomfortable turn. I am leaving here right now!"

"Please Miss Reilly, calm down. Let me finish explaining. You see, our organization has been grooming you for years, because of your background, your research, your philosophical attitude, your energy and your willingness to reach out for information."

"What organization are we talking about? Who are these people?"

"I can only tell you that my contact is reliable but that I do not know the identity of the persons at the top. You should know that your friend, David Schilling, is also a trusted and chosen one."

Nancy sat back in her chair and relaxed slightly. "I am afraid you are overwhelming me, Mr. Verneau. I am not a member of any organization except professional ones devoted to library science and history."

"Operatives of significant events in history are often appointed only to carry out specific assignments, without knowledge of the larger organization."

Nancy looked at Verneau sharply. "Are you suggesting that I have an assignment? My purpose in being here is simply to gain knowledge and to collect information for my library and my doctorate program."

"There is a larger purpose, here, Miss Reilly. May I have your pledge of secrecy so that we may go on?"

"I don't know why I should agree to any of this. I don't know you at all."

"Your daughter, Ruth, is in the Catskill Mountains in New York with her father. Is she safe?"

Nancy jumped up. "How could you possibly know that?"

"Please understand that we have a common purpose and that if I have that information, so might the evil forces that would like to find her."

Nancy sat back down, and her hands began to tremble. "Mr. Verneau, there is nothing in this world more important to me than my daughter. You have made me horribly frightened."

"Miss Reilly I can assure you she is safe. Our people are watching out for her safety as we speak."

"How can I be assured of that?" said Nancy in an anxious voice.

"I can put you in touch with David Schilling. Do you trust him?"

"Why yes but how can he know about this?"

"He has been contacted by a ranking member of the Freemasonry organization and has agreed to help."

———

Thinking back over the Paris episode, the documents revealed by Mr. Verneau, and the brief conversation with David Schilling by a filtered phone call, Nancy was even more eager to get to Rome for her meeting with Monsignor Averti. This was a two and one half hour flight so she would have some time to relax before she arrived in the city. David had verified that he was completing his plans to meet her and that he would contact her at her hotel. While he had assured her that Ruth was safe, he cautioned her about meeting with Monsignor Averti before they had a chance to talk.

CHAPTER 33

▼

DAVID'S PREPARATION, TRIP TO EUROPE, ADVENTURE IN ROME

David zippered his suit case and rolled it into the garage for loading into the Suburban. His lap top computer had gone through the closing procedure. He removed it from the docking port and secured it in his carry on bag. His house sitter would be here tonight to take care of his cat, Yogi, and to watch over the house in his absence.

Leaving the village, he was eager to make his trip to Rome, but was also wistfully thinking about his return and the completion of his book in the safety and peace of his home. The call from The Grand Master had shocked him with surprise. He had made a quick two day trip to New York to satisfy himself that all was well with Ruth and her father, Frank, in the Catskills.

He wished that air travel did not prevent him from carrying his small but effective twenty two caliber pistol. He had worked on his proficiency with fire arms for years and felt quite comfortable with guns. This was becoming impractical, though, with new laws and the terrorist activity making it difficult to carry.

Fire arms had been necessary at times because of the threats arising from his construction projects.

His Karate lessons had stopped short of advance certification but left him with proficient tools for self protection. The great thing was that Karate provided aerobic exercise and a sharpening of his physical senses.

He stopped at the carry-out for two shredded chicken sandwiches to eat on the way to the airport. It would be a while before he could get this kind of food, including cheese burgers. Comfort food was one of the things he missed most on his trips around the world.

Driving past his former company headquarters, he thought about the excitement and the anxiety of his real estate ventures. While it had provided him with a good living, and freedom, it had to be steered, hands-on, daily. He didn't miss that part. This thinking led him into recollections of his relationships with the women in his life. It seemed that he was just destined to live alone. He enjoyed the company of women but seemed to rapidly become uncomfortable with co-habiting. The mother of his children was a good woman, but they just couldn't co-exist over the long term. He was thankful, though, that they were still friends, even though she was re-married. He had had a brief second marriage with a lovely woman but mutually agreed that the long term was not working. He didn't know how to analyze this about himself but he was extremely wary about another marriage.

Manhattan and the Statue of Liberty were visible because of the departure pattern of the Boeing 757 from La Guardia airport. David looked out the window finding it hard to imagine that seven million people lived on that small island and its metropolitan surroundings. The cleared site of the World Trade Center stood out because of its emptiness. The attack of 9/11 that destroyed the Towers and killed thousands of persons, brought the reality of the harsh world of religion and ideology home, and into focus, rather than the reporting of television and the newspapers from distant countries. Power, for whatever reason, always seems to take away resources from some, while accumulating for others. Death and tragedy, a by product of the quest for power, is a necessity, not an option. David realized that he could not point a finger at any group as the assassins, since all have killed at one time or another throughout history, for their beliefs.

His economics studies at Ohio State had pointed out statistical data that proved the six billion persons on our globe, were fighting for resources that could serve only a much smaller number. Superstition and ignorance only complicates the problem and makes it worse.

While he was thinking about work ethic and the distribution of world power and resources; the problem seemed hopeless; he became drowsy and drifted off into a deep sleep. With the help of a sleeping pill that he took only on long flights, he woke up and realized he was only two hours from a quick stop in Paris to catch the final leg of his flight to Rome.

————

"Senor are you spending much time in Rome?" David looked up from his guide booklet of Rome and the Vatican. A beautiful dark eyed flight attendant was looking over his shoulder. She was in her early twenties, well built and smiling.

"Why yes, about two weeks." He smiled back, "I didn't realize you were standing there. Are you based in Rome?"

"Yes, have you been there before?"

"No, this will be my first time. I plan to spend several days at the Vatican studying for the book I am writing."

"Oh, you are an author?"

He wondered why she had time to chat, but when he looked around the first class cabin, he realized that many of the seats were empty.

"I don't know if you could call me an author, yet. I have had only a few minor things published. You speak English very well. I assume that you are Italian."

"Yes and I am studying for my degree at the University."

"How do you find time for school with this job as a flight attendant?"

"The University of Malta, the Link Campus has a very flexible program. Its instruction language is in English. I am going there so I may learn another language."

"What course of study are you taking?"

"International studies and museum history. This course work allows me to be a licensed tourist guide as part of the curriculum."

David was intrigued. "You must have no time for yourself with your job and school."

"I am busy, yes, but the program is so exciting and allows me much diversity. Do you have a guide in Rome?"

"Well no, but perhaps I should. I really do waste a lot of time when I travel because of being so independent."

"If you would like to hear about our services I would be happy to take you to our agency in Rome."

"You know, that might really be a good idea. I am feeling overwhelmed by the number of things I want to see and do."

———

With a few days of time before Nancy's arrival, I enjoyed a luxurious breakfast buffet in the Regina Balboni hotel dining room and then went to the concierge desk. The man was professional and studious looking. When I asked, "Parla Inglese senor," he smiled and said, "Yes sir. How may I help you?"

"I would like to find an English speaking guide that can take me to see some landmarks and explain the history of Rome."

He thought for a moment. "Are you interested in a personal guide?"

"Yes, it is just me."

"Ah, that would be Roberto. Would you like for me to call him for you?"

"Yes, that would be wonderful. Thank you very much."

In the short time I have been here I have already learned that there is a significant difference between the pronunciations of similar words in Italian versus Spanish. In Spanish, thank you is Gracias, but in Italian it is Grazie. Even with the Berlitz Phrase book I could not say "Graatseeay" with confidence. So with all the English speaking people here I just revert to my own language. I am somewhat concerned about the audacity of Americans to fear mistakes and ridicule but I continue, nevertheless.

Roberto is the owner of the agency, Gilberto did the first half day driving tour to acquaint me with the general outline of the city, and Alberto turned out to be my guide for the week. I wondered if there were any Tonys or Harrys in Italy or if everyone had an "erto" suffix to their names.

A guide, arranged by my travel agent, had met me at the gate upon arrival at Leonardo DaVinci airport and took me directly to the Catacombs at San Callisto, at the beginning of the morning. This is a ninety acre pastoral area, like an Ohio farm, with sheep and cows grazing, and beautiful flora adorning the landscape. I was grateful to find a bathroom, after the nine hour flight, but otherwise, I felt alert after flying all night.

We drove over one of the original sections of the Apian Way not far from the entrance. This was the beginning of my realization of the antiquity of every surface and above and below ground fabrication in Rome. The stones of the highway may have been in place for two thousand years as a result of the emperor's effort to "have all roads lead to Rome." This was so important to communications when smoke signals, mirrors, flags, pigeons, and couriers were the primary means of sending information over long distances. Of equal importance, the transportation of produce, crafted goods, and trade items, of all types, was made possible by wide, paved roads allowing horses, and wagons to travel without fear of mud, rock slides, and other impediments. Robbers and bandits were thwarted because of the Roman's ability to patrol and guard the highway. And the Roman armies could move quickly over it when needed.

My "English Speaking" guide's presentation, at the Catacombs, was truly a parody of someone speaking a language with which they were very uncomfortable. She finished almost every word with "A" like you might see a stand up comedian doing in an Italian impression. Her words and sentence structure were fine but the syllables and the inability to convert the alphabet, made her presentation almost useless. I did, however get the general idea of the centuries old history of the catacombs. With the four levels and the endless corridors, and stairs, someone could be lost here, forever, in the darkness, without light, a guide or a map. Some Popes and other important people had been laid to rest here

The Regina Balboni is an old world European hotel on the Via Vittorio Veneto, a street that ended at the gates of the "Walled City". These walls extend for thirteen miles around ancient Rome. I could walk two blocks to the City Gates and across the street to Villa Borghese, the estate of a wealthy family—one an influential Cardinal, now a museum and park area. The "Via Veneto" is a street where the entertainment celebrities stay. Pictures of Frank Sinatra and Dean Martin are common. The background music at the hotel was mainly of these two. I was to spend four days, here, before my move to the Alante Star Hotel near the Vatican. Nancy would be arriving soon after.

The Italian marble throughout the hotel, including my bathroom, is an enduring source of enjoyment, to me, as an American. It probably is common place to Romans, though, because the marble is everywhere in the City. Even the Coliseum was at one time covered with Travertine marble as a veneer over the stone structure. Succeeding emperors pirated the marble for other buildings of their own design. This was a custom of Kings, Popes, and Emperors.

The marble, the cobblestone streets and other hard surfaces, all contributed to the arthritis in my aching knees. I spent much time looking for the rare presence of soft carpet.

————

"Alberto, Stop! My head is about to burst." I gestured by whirling my fingers around my ears to add emphasis.

Startled, he looked at me without saying any thing.

"Alberto, you are knowledgeable and I am a willing student, but my ability to absorb all the visual and spoken information is causing a great strain on my brain."

"Mr. Schilling, I am sorry, there is so much to tell. Please let me know if we are going too fast."

"It is all right," I said. "I just need to go a little slower. My knees have been giving me pain because of the wet weather bothering my arthritis."

With a concerned look, Alberto said, "I struggle with the refinements of the English language. Perhaps I am too, shall I say, zealous, with trying to compress all my learning into a few hours of instruction."

"Alberto, please, I assure you that you are doing a wonderful job and I really want the information."

We were standing in Saint Peter's Basilica in front of a mosaic work of art. He was going into great detail while I was looking off in the distance at a large canopy in the center of the rotunda. And then there was just my sheer awe at the gold, the clear span design and all the adornments, everywhere I looked. I wanted to pause there and drink it in. I have spent a lifetime hearing about the Vatican, and now I am here. I want to enjoy the moment.

I can not do justice to a description of Saint Peter's Basilica, the Sistine Chapel, the Vatican Museum and the concept of the entire Vatican country. Alberto explained, "Mr. Schilling we are now leaving Italy and crossing over into the sovereign country of the Vatican."

I looked across the vast paved area towards Saint Peters and felt the boundaries of the country enclosed by the statuary on either side. This was a cobblestone area, with a fountain near the entry.

The Swiss Guard, the official guard, selected from the Swiss Army was visible at only one location. "Mr. Schilling these are—."

I cut him off. "Please call me David, Alberto."

"Dahveed, these soldiers are hand picked guards for the Vatican country. Those uniforms were personally designed by Michelangelo in the sixteenth century. The men all have to be very similar in size and skill level."

They certainly didn't look very menacing to me. The pantaloons were striped in a orange and blue and their hats like in a version of a Shakespearian play. I wondered, *how could they possibly protect all the countless billions of dollars of treasure, here in the Vatican.*

"David, if you look up at the window on the third floor you can see where the Pope holds audience every Wednesday morning." He was pointing. I looked up but it seemed a long ways from where we were standing. I wondered how you could actually see the Pope.

———

I checked into the Regina Balboni Hotel. The room was clean and spacious in an old world style. I found a port for my laptop computer and an electrical outlet with the proper voltage. After quickly unpacking and freshening up I took the elevator to the lobby floor and followed the signs to the patio dining area. The view of Rome got my juices flowing and added to the sense of frustration of knowing all the places to go and the things to see in Italy. Just the guidebooks of Rome, Milan, Florence, Venice; the cradle of the depictions of Michelangelo, DaVinci, and the preservation of monuments to the struggles of the Christian world and the battles with the world around it, overwhelmed me. How could I possibly have enough energy to satisfy my quest for adventure and knowledge? *I must spend my time wisely. The Vatican; how can I do this properly before my meetings with Nancy and Dominick Averti?*

Sipping a glass of wine, while enjoying a light snack, calmed me down. *I need to take it easy on alcohol so that I don't get sleepy and miss the night life here.* I had a tendency to have a couple of drinks late in the afternoon or early evening and say, "To heck with night life," and go home to bed. With that thought, I took the flight attendant's card from my pocket. Gloria Peole—that sounded like a combination of American and Spanish rather than Italian. While recalling her beauty and the effect that beautiful women had on me, I tried to get in touch with my practical senses. She was too young and this would only end up in frustration for me.

I was surprised to find the message light blinking on my telephone when I went to the room for my map and camera. "Mr. Schilling, Hi it is Gloria. If you are interested in a guided tour please call me at the number on my card. I am very familiar with the Vatican but will be out of town for the next three days. Please call me if you are interested."

"Now what?" I was wrestling with my judgment. I often talked out loud to myself when I did that. *Don't do something stupid you dumb ass!*

———

After a long day of walking my thoughts were: *One, You must be very strong to be a tourist here. Two, men and women alike seem to wear only black suits. Three, History is not a straight line. Four, A simple jacket for dinner can cost 2,600 Euro or about $3,500.* I was sent to the Brioni department store by the concierge from my hotel, after being rejected from entry to a restaurant because the doorman didn't like my jacket. I am not a penny pincher but I was shocked at the prices. When I asked my guide, who could afford to shop at Brioni, he said, "Oil rich Arabs come here without any concern about money and may spend $40,000 just to go out for the evening."

My impression is that the Italians are friendly and very busy. The street traffic is frenzied but not that different from home, where the most dangerous condition is a 110# girl driving a three ton Ford Excursion, while talking on a mobile phone, applying lipstick, looming just a few feet from my bumper. I am haunted by that picture, from my rear view mirror, even in my sleep.

Romulous, the Ceasars, Hadrian; Greek, Jewish, Arab and other conquerors, all, left their respective marks on Rome. Much of this is still here today.

Hadrian's statue in the Vatican reminded me of a high school sports hero that used his fame to have sex with every desirable girl in his universe. His curly hair partly hid prominent ears and made him look rather benign in contrast to the bully with enormous energy who left structures, and bodies, all over Europe.

Surprisingly, he is depicted as a homosexual along with statues of his boy friends. His history indicated that he could be friendly but not a friend. He died at age 39.

The Sistine Chapel with man's version of the evolution of civilization, the creation of life forms and the foundation of Christianity are displayed by the genius of Michelangelo, Raphael, and their pupils, peers and teachers. The two worked within shouting proximity of each other at the Vatican.

Alberto, my eager guide, touched my arm, "Please David we should wait for a moment. We can sit here on the bench."

What's up now? I thought. I was relieved to sit a minute after walking on marble and cobblestones all day.

He spoke to a friend of his at a book stand in one of the great galleries leading into the Sistine Chapel and returned to me with a bound book filled with glorious photographs of the Vatican City.

Tourists from every country filed past with flashing cameras assaulting the hanging paintings and frescoes. I thought, *the energy from all these cameras throughout the world could send a rocket ship to the moon. What a waste! Most of the photos will end up in a box never to be seen again.*

Mesmerized by watching the hordes of tourists, my ear was still not tuned to my name being pronounced as Dahveed, so I didn't hear Alberto, at first, "David we need to review what you are going to see when you go into the Chapel. I can't talk with you in there, because there is a strict policy of silence."

Michelangelo's work in that room is beyond description. We focused on the ceiling panels depicting the creations of the earth, Adam, Eve, the Ascension and many other things, that I was taught in my Bible study classes at the Methodist Church, as a child.

I entered the Chapel in an attitude of the strict Methodist teaching of humility only to be greeted by a room packed with people, whispering and talking to each other as if at a giant cocktail party. My annoyance grew as I walked around the Chapel looking for a place to sit so that I could focus on the Master's artwork and the attitude of absorption of the Christian principles learned from my childhood until now. Standing, looking up forty to fifty feet was not the best position for viewing scenes from concepts so important to history.

Finally, a bench seat at the wall opened and I quickly claimed it. I was trying to close out the distractions from the two or three hundred unruly tourists to begin my appreciation of the work overhead. From the corner of my eye I saw a very attractive young woman approach. She sat down right next to me.

No God Damn it! I am not going to think about an attractive woman. Stop, you can't swear in here. Focus, David, focus!

"Hello, can you hear me?"

I heard this voice. Who the Hell can that be?

I looked to my right. The attractive woman was talking on a cell phone in the Sistine Chapel, the Sistine Chapel!

My quiet anger rose to the point that I could picture her as one of the Christian sacrifices at Circus Maximus with three hundred thousand cheering spectators.

When she stopped talking and put the cell phone in her handbag, I couldn't resist asking her, "Who were you calling, the Pope?"

She was totally oblivious. "That would be nice," she said.

This was one of the few Americans that I met in Rome. I can see why the adjective, "ugly" is attached to us.

Rome is unlike any other city I have visited. Although there was destruction by early conquerors, even the Nazi looters and the Allies refused to bomb the city during World War II. This, like Paris, was declared an "Open City"

While my mission, here, is to search the Vatican and later use my special appointment to enter its archives, in hopes of acquiring access to information not available to outsiders, it is imperative that I touch and feel Rome, first hand, in my travels about the city.

I could be distracted by the beautiful and engaging young women and confess that my inscriptions from that subject are not necessarily bound by historic accuracy.

Again, I had to appeal to Alberto to slow down. His fast walking pace had already moved him yards in front of me.

"Are you all right, Mr. Schilling?" He turned from many paces ahead to look back at me.

"I am fine but this wet, rainy weather has agitated the arthritis in my knees."

Various sports injuries from football, basketball, tennis, running, and skiing have contributed to knee stress over the years. The floors and streets in Rome are marble, cobblestone, asphaltic concrete. There are few soft surfaces. Walking and standing all day are in direct conflict with my curiosity and endurance.

"David you may cure your pain by losing weight. You know, low fat, no sugars, no bread, no pasta."

"Alberto I have practiced that prison sentence in the past but have been very lax, lately."

Shit! I am tired of stopping to rest my knees at all hours of the day. God Damn it, I am going back to a severe diet when I get home. I am sick of squeezing into trousers with my underwear up my butt all day.

————

Gianni and Gabriel are stewards in the lounge at the hotel. Gianni is 39 and lives across the country on the Adriatic coast. He goes home each week to be with his 28 year old girl friend. I was having trouble understanding his first name. He picked a bottle of Johnnie Walker scotch and said, "Gianni like Johnny Walker." So I called him Johnny Walker from then on. While Gianni has been here four years, Gabriel has been here 40 years. They became my best friends, while sharing many stories about the hotel, in particular, the Arabs, prostitutes—20 years ago, and the movie stars that stayed here.

As I waited in the lounge for the 7:30 dinner hour, Gabriel answered my questions about the country. "Chinese, Albanian, Polish Mafia come here illegally. Moroccans, Africans come by boat to Sicily and sneak behind Italian navy patrol boats. So many here without jobs, must steal to live. They use our hospitals. I pay."

"Gabriel, we have the same problem in my country with illegal aliens."

We discussed the European common market and the Euro versus the old Italian Lira and the U.S. Dollar. The Euro seems like a good idea to me, as a tourist, but I sensed that Gabriel misses the Lira. If the United States, Canada and Mexico could establish a common currency, who would benefit? I am not sure if NAFTA is a benefit or a curse, or if it creates some of the same issues as the European Common Market.

––––––––

"Alberto, where does the money come from to maintain all the antiquities in Rome? Churches, Statues, fountains, palaces, buildings, ruins like the Forum, the Colosseum, Circus Maximus, it seems impossible?"

Without hesitation he said, "Roma is a museum for the World; a museum without walls. Money comes from everywhere."

With my business education and experience, and a lifetime of budgeting, I raised my eyebrows but said nothing.

"Mr. Schilling"—

"Alberto please call me David."

"Yes, Dahveed."

"It's all right. I can't pronounce your last name either."

"Circus Maximus could seat up to 320,000 people. 35,000 Christians were massacred there."

"I thought the Colosseum was used for that," I said in surprise.

"The Colosseum was used more for entertainment than for executions. The Emperor knew that if he could entertain people, and supply them with food and drink, it would take their minds off their problems and reduce the risk of rebellion."

"Alberto, we do the same thing with our football games in the U.S."

He looked at me in disbelief.

I continued, "The similarity is that our players are almost always injured or crippled. In some cases the athletes die."

He started to say something but I knew I had to keep going in order to get a word in.

"We have 50,000 to over 100,000 people go to watch these games. They eat, they get drunk, they express hatred for their team's opponent. They scream, 'kill them' and they pay big sums of money to do this. Almost everyone wears battle gear."

He was giving me a look of skepticism.

"My theory is that this is a substitute for battles and wars. Our people use this as a diversion from other forms of violence."

"I see," said Alberto without much conviction.

———

When I visited the Museum at Borghese Villa, I decided to go on my own without a guide. I walked from my hotel to the ancient city gates, but instead of going through there and across the street to the Villa, I took a tunnel walkway to the Borghese grounds. When I emerged, I was totally disoriented and could not figure out where I was located on this vast estate.

My 10:00 appointment to enter the museum was only about 10 minutes away but I could walk that far in any direction and be completely wrong. I kept trying to catch someone's eye to stop them and ask directions but everyone was hurrying by. Finally, I stopped a woman who looked at me and slowed her step. She was young, blonde, medium height and slim. She smiled, spoke in English, then pointed down a path to the museum and took off in another direction. She said she was from London.

Fortunately I arrived at the museum doors with about two minutes to spare. The woman from London arrived at the entrance at the same time. I have no idea why she directed me differently.

As it turned out she was in my group of three with an English speaking guide. My assumption was that she was friendly and that we would converse during the tour. Instead she became completely frigid. I could only think that I must have reminded her of a former husband.

The most memorable art work from my entire time in Rome was here, the statue by Bernini, [1598—1680] "Apollo and Daphne." This depicts the nymph Daphne being turned into a laurel tree while pursued in vain by Apollo. She was such a beauty but she rejected Apollo, the Archer, God of medicine prophecy and music, as she did all others. The fine detail of the body features and the fabrics, sculpted in marble, caused me to pause here for several minutes.

———

On my last night at the hotel before transferring to the Alante Star, I had a few drinks in the bar while chatting with my new friends. I got up to walk outside to smoke a cigar in front of the hotel. It was reasonably chilly and I was standing near the wall of the building on a public sidewalk, near the entrance. The moist, cool, air caused me to realize how much I had drunk, on an empty stomach. I was feeling tipsy.

A woman walked up to me and said, "You like to have drink? I introduce you to woman." She was short, older, and looked like someone you might see cleaning the hallways.

I looked at her and thought, *Oh no! I am not falling for this old trick, particularly not in a foreign country.*

The next thing I knew the words, "Okay. Where?" involuntarily came out of my mouth. There was obviously a short circuit to the brain.

She grabbed my hand and started me around the corner to a lighted sign indicating a night club in the lower level.

We went down a wide curving staircase to view a dance floor, a large band stand, a bar, and were met by a smiling maitre d'. She spoke a few words to him, then he ushered us to a couch with a cocktail table.

She got up from the couch and said, "I be right back."

The danger signals were beginning to go off in my head. The lights in the club we very dim but I could see that there were few other people here.

She returned with a beautiful young woman. She was dressed like a professional business person, in a form fitting suit. Simultaneously a waiter appeared and asked if we wanted wine. All this was happening very quickly. I said, "Of course," but now a sense of reason was beginning to creep into my mind.

That all went away when she smiled, took my hand, and leaned close. In very good English she asked me, "Where are you staying? Are you in Rome for long?"

I was now looking at her long shapely legs and the very prominent breasts straining against the buttons of her jacket. She had light amber skin, dark hair and a beautifully fine featured face.

"I am staying in the hotel around the corner and this is my last night. By the way, what is the cost of the wine, here."

She smiled and said, "About eighty Euro, I think."

"Oh, okay," I stammered. *That's about one hundred and ten dollars, I thought. What the Hell!*

The first bottle of wine arrived and then the second. By this time we were talking about my hotel room and price. I paid with a credit card, yes, a credit card in a clip joint. It was so dark I could not see the total.

We went in the front entrance of my hotel. Even in my drunken state, I was feeling slightly sheepish about this.

She said, "I have to check in at the desk."

Oh God no! I thought.

There stood the stern faced concierge, the same one that sent me to buy a $3,500 jacket. I felt like I had just been caught hiding in a closed stall at the girl's rest room in my high school or in the classroom with no clothing.

I looked to the outside and thought for a moment that I saw the same blonde English woman, whom I met at the Borghese Villa, walk by and look in. No, J must be imagining things. *Forget it. No one here is ever going to see you again.*

After a few dark looks from the concierge and feeling as if I were center stage in the brilliant lighting at Rockefeller Center, she came to where I was standing at the elevator.

Even in my alcohol impaired state, when she took off her clothes, I could only stare at her honey colored skin and the flawless features of her face and body.

Barely able to squeak out words, I asked, "Where are you from?"

"Jamaica," she said.

I thought of lots of other questions but decided to pay attention to the subject, at hand, instead.

Thank God, I was too impaired to get in further trouble, but I did compare her to the statue of Daphne at the Borghese museum and was satisfied how perfect and desirable a woman can look. It occurred to me that Daphne's sculptor could not have been homosexual, because of the appreciation, if not lust, when he detailed her body.

———

The next morning as I checked out of The Regina Balboni, I handed the concierge an envelope with money for his services during my stay. He smiled and was very pleasant as if the events of last night were either not observed or completely forgotten.

The limousine was waiting at the entrance. My bags had already been sent to the Alante Star hotel. The smiling doorman held the door and accepted the offered tip. I had checked out, said my good byes to the staff, and left tips for the dining room manager and the bellman. They had really contributed to the comfort of my stay. I am not sure how approving of me they were because of some of my actions and companions.

It was raining as the driver of the big black Mercedes—Benz sedan, held open the door for me. He seemed friendly. I mumbled from the back seat, "It has rained for three of my four days here."

His abrupt indifference to my remarks signaled that I was in for a silent ride to the new hotel. *Fine with me.*

Sunday morning traffic was sparse leaving me with a feeling of aloneness. We drove past antiquities on every corner. The driver was accelerating his speed threatening pedestrians, cars, motor scooters and making me feel very uncomfortable.

Many of the streets are narrow or one—way leaving very little room to pass. He turned onto a back street and then another.

He must be taking a short cut to the main street. This doesn't look right at all!

He started down a hill in an alley, then, made a sharp turn to right to be faced with a triangular shaped building in a very dark paved area, at a fork in the street. The road to the left was blocked by a large van. The road to the right was blocked by a service vehicle. The driver brought the sedan to an abrupt stop and just sat there, staring ahead.

What the Hell? Where were we? I was getting very angry with this person.

He turned slowly, completely around in his seat and pointed a hand gun at me. "You get out here," he said with a look of indifference.

"What are you doing?" My immediate thought was to bolt out the door and run but when I grabbed the handle it was locked. Then two men, one at each passenger door, appeared with guns.

"You get out, now!"

With three guns pointed at me, I had no choices. My heart was pounding like a piston and my knees were weak, hardly supporting me. I have never pissed myself in fear, before, but felt I was about to.

"What is this? Who are you people?"

"You come," said one of the men in a guttural voice, as he grabbed my arm, roughly, and pushed me towards an open doorway. The man on my left had my other arm. I was thrust into a dark hallway, with stone floors, and heard the reinforced wooden door slam shut behind me.

My God! No one has any idea where I am. I stood alone in the dark musty hallway, a prisoner behind locked doors, with no contact to the outside world.

I stood still for a while trying to adjust my eyes to the darkness. There was the faint sound of voices outside the door. One sounded like a woman. From a small crack where the wooden door planks met, I could see the two men, the driver, and a woman. It looked like the same woman I saw at the Villa Borghese. They were talking with hand gestures and great animation. They seemed to be arguing, then, they all looked towards the door where I was imprisoned. One of the men broke away and started towards my location. I thought, *they are going to realize their mistake and let me out of here. There is going to be Hell for them to pay when I go to the police.*

Feeling hopeful I was startled when another door, apparently an outside one, slammed shut over the one I was looking through. I could hear the latching and locking. Now I was encased in total pitch blackness and could hear nothing from the outside world.

For a few minutes I didn't move, fearful of what ever else might be in the room or corridor. After a time, hearing and seeing nothing, I began to inch my way around the area, taking baby steps and feeling the walls with my hands. It was very stuffy in here causing me to perspire.

After making a complete round from the door where I started and back again, I found that all the surfaces were stone except for another doorway that was closed with planking inches thick. I pounded on these planks but my blows were met with a dull thud, as if a masonry wall was on the other side.

As high as I could reach, only the stone wall could be detected. Even with jumping as high as I could there was no change. There was nothing to stand on and nothing to climb so I could not get to the ceiling.

After about an hour of probing I finally sat down on the stone floor. The surface was stone and cold to the touch. I listened but could not hear a sound. I tried yelling but the echo in the room was the only response.

I sat there for several more minutes trying to piece together the events of the past several days and weeks. Was I being pursued by the same people that murdered Otto Henlein at the Castle Inn in Bavaria? What would they want with me? How did the blonde woman from the Villa Borghese fit in? Was the Jamaican at my hotel part of a plot?

After several hours passed, I had actually dosed off while sitting on the stone floor. I woke up, cold, hungry, frightened and in dire need of a bathroom. I decided to crawl slowly over the floor surfaces to further survey my cell like surroundings. After about thirty minutes of this my knees were bruised and my hands were chafed. Again, I sat with my back to the wall, thinking about what I could do next.

At one point during my crawling probe, there was kind of a hollow sound or feel over an area where the floor was made up of larger flat paving stones. I crawled back in that direction guided by the reference to the entry door at my back. Finally I came upon that area after stopping to tap the floor with the heel of my hand in several places. The hollow sound seemed to center around one particularly large stone. I leaned over and placed my ear to the stone. It was almost as if I could hear or sense water, or a tunnel. I wasn't sure which.

I don't know if you can ever get completely accustomed to the dark but I was feeling more in charge of my surroundings, the longer I was here. My wrist watch, with powerful luminance for the dark places in underwater scuba diving, was like a beacon in the blackness.

While holding the watch near the joint in the larger stone, I thought I could detect a crack or slightly wider area than near the other ones. As I tapped continuously around the area, it became more and more apparent that there was a hollow area under the large stone. I tried to pry on this with my finger tips, with no success. Pounding harder with the heel of my hand accomplished nothing. Finally I stood straight up with great difficulty because of the lack of reference with sight to walls, light or ceiling. My stability, with nothing to hold on to, was shaky.

I succeeded in standing directly over the large stone and began to pound it with my foot. The heavy shoes I was wearing dislodged the stone to the point I could feel a ridge sticking up above the adjoining ones. I got back to my knees and with great difficulty was able to pry the stone further upward. Then, I slid it over to find an opening about three feet wide. It made me think of a manhole cover. I cautiously extended my hand and then my arm in the abyss, fearful of what lie down there.

Why my reading and the comments from one of my guides came to mind, I don't know. Before I came to Rome I had been reading a book about Pompeii and its volcanic destruction from the eruption of Mount Vesuvius, almost two thousand years ago. The major subject of the book was about the aqueduct system that fed fresh water from the mountains to Rome, Pompeii and other cities. The engineering from that early period was beyond belief although I had seen much other evidence of the advance of technology from ancient times, such as the pyramids.

I thought of all the beautiful fountains in Rome and the instruction from my guide that 90% of all the fountains were still fed by the aqueduct system built before the time of Christ.

Necessity began to overcome fear. This opening in the floor was the only venue to movement out of this prison of a room. Thinking of all the horror movies I have seen and of the possibility of creatures of the dark, I lowered myself into the hole. I was surprised when I found bottom only shoulder deep.

I lowered myself and with my hands could feel the openings on either side of where I was kneeling. As I cautiously moved my hands to detect the size and surface of this cavern, it seemed, incredibly, that this was a tunnel about three feet in diameter. To my left there was no sound but to my right, I thought I could hear the very faint sound of traffic noise.

Again, I thought of the ancient aqueduct builders and the advanced technology that I had read about. Feet first, I crept forward in the tunnel towards the sound. I was envisioning all kinds of creatures in this dark hole, but I had no other choice than to proceed. As I rounded a bend in the tunnel I could see light in the distance. Encouraged, I covered the last few yards quickly and found myself looking to the outside in full daylight. The opening was blocked by a steel grating.

I managed to turn myself around so that I could see out and found myself looking out into space, over the ancient Forum. I turned again so that my feet were against the grating and kicked at the metal structure. Surprisingly, the grating began to give way rather easily. I kicked until it fell away completely. There was a loud clatter as the grating fell several yards and landed on what sounded like a stone surface.

Turning again, I peered out the opening into the ruins, that were off limits to tourists and accessible only to archeologists. Of course, no one was around on a Sunday morning. Undetected, I stepped out onto a ledge at my right. Miraculously, there was a walkway right up to the street.

I stepped out and looked back over where I had escaped from. It was clearly the remnants of the old aqueduct system, high above the Forum. This accounted for the tunnel's absence of debris and rodents.

Concerned about my abductors, I moved close to a wall, pulled out my map of Rome to get my bearings, and found that I was only walking distance to the Hotel Alante Star. There was no sign of any one watching me. I stayed close to walls and buildings and walked to the hotel. *I must spend the rest of my time in Rome looking over my shoulder, in fear, and questioning every encounter with strangers.*

CHAPTER 34

▼

MARIA AT THE CASTLE INN—BAVARIA

Angelina stood on the sidewalk, with a worried look, while Maria drove away, with the top down, in her sports car. She stood there, motionless, even after Maria was out of sight. *How much do I dare tell her? She is a beautiful, intelligent child and deserves to know the truth about her background. Would it destroy her?* With a sigh and a shrug, Angelina walked back up the stairs to the pension.

———

Maria walked in the front door of the Castle Inn, and as luck would have it, there stood Lotar Herron at the front desk. He looked up, surprised, "Maria Albrecht, what are you doing here? I have wanted to talk with you."

She didn't notice that she was being followed for the one and one half hour drive from the village to the castle. Guido was excellent at stalking without being detected. He watched her turn into the Castle Inn and then drove on past to a hiding place.

Lotar and Maria sat alone in the patio restaurant, talking about the events that they had encountered. Maria had many questions about the murder here, the mysterious event of Bishop Rhein's disappearance and the secrecy of the Abby at Etal.

"There is so much to tell you, child. I don't know where to begin."

"Please Mr. Herron; I am not a child. I have a right to know the answers to all these things."

"I am sorry. Of course you have that right. First, let me caution you; it is not safe to go searching for answers at the Abby. The Cathedral in your village has a great deal of secret information and was a safe place while Bishop Rhein was there. Now it is not safe either."

Maria was listening, intently, when the alarms to the hotel started blaring furiously. Lotar excused himself and ran to investigate.

Guido had crept through the woods to the mechanical room of the Castle, which was poorly secured. He was inside in an instant and set the alarm in motion. It not only made a loud racket at the hotel but was wired into the police station.

Lotar returned to the patio to Maria. "Miss Albrecht I am sorry, I must go to the village immediately to tell them it was a false alarm so that they don't send the police up here. I will talk with you when I return."

Maria went to her room to take a shower, then, just sat there impatiently, wondering what to do next. It was getting dark outside in the late summer evening. She was startled by a knock at her door. There was no one there, so she walked into the hallway and saw the entrance to the Medieval Castle where she and David had had the encounter. It appeared that the entrance door was ajar. *How could this be? That place is under tight security.*

She slowly opened the door and saw no one. She cautiously stepped inside and to her surprise the door closed tightly behind her. She tried to open the door but it wouldn't move. There was just enough light to see the outline of objects on the floor below her. All she could think about was a castle dungeon as she descended the stairs. Maybe there was another way out of here.

She walked slowly in the low light to an area that was slightly illuminated. Suddenly, she was grabbed from behind with a hand over her mouth so she could not scream. Her arms were pinned tightly behind her. She felt herself growing faint from the anesthetic at her mouth and nostrils.

Guido was naked from the waist down and erect from the excitement and anticipation.

When Maria awoke she was shackled to the medieval instruments with all her clothes removed and a gag in her mouth.

The dark swarthy man laughed in a low guttural sound and tweaked the nipples of her breasts. "Now my beauty, you are mine."

Trying to scream, stifled, with the gag in her mouth almost made her pass out again.

He had a whip in his hand and his member was extended, dark and ugly. He ran his hands over and into her body. She saw other tools of torture on the table beside him.

Maria thought, *this is how my life is going to end by being raped and tortured by a medieval beast.*

He stepped back, laughed, picked up some other tools, and approached her. She could smell his fetid breath. Her entire life passed through her consciousness knowing she was going to die. In her anxiety with her red hair over her shoulders, and her fair skin outlining the pubic area and her nipples, she was even more desirable. Guido was ecstatic over having his way with someone with such beauty.

At a time like this I am surprised at my regret, not of my imminent death but of all the unanswered questions in my life. She experienced a great sadness, overpowering her fear that this monster was going to take away the happiness and excitement of the rest of her life.

As he came closer with unidentified implements in his hands, she struggled out of reflex in spite of knowing there was no use.

Guido's eyes were wide with excitement. He was just a few inches from her face. She could feel his disgusting member against her body. His eyes grew wider, then, he looked up at the ceiling as his mouth opened as if to groan in ecstasy. He hesitated and dropped his arms. From the dimness behind him she could see fingers around Guido's throat. He finally closed his eyes and his lifeless body dropped to the floor.

There stood Lotar Herron, towering over her, wearing a white tunic with a red cross on the front. He held his huge farmers hands out in front of him. He grabbed a blanket and covered her and then unfastened her hands and legs from the irons.

She was resting in her room when the police came. It was the same inspector Houser that had investigated the murder of Dr. Otto Heinlin. This time he was much more friendly and sympathetic. After considering the similarity of Maria and Lotar's stories he determined that there would be no charges and that the investigation was finished other than finding the identity of Guido.

Later that day, Maria and Lotar were talking about the experiences. "If I just had some idea if Bishop Rhein is still alive, there are so many things I would like to ask him," said Maria.

Lotar was silent at the mention of Bishop Rhein. He thought for a moment, then, said, "Bishop Rhein is alive. I can take you to him."

CHAPTER 35

▼

OPUS DEI HEADQUARTERS, NEW YORK

The Bishop was standing, frozen in place, looking at the report of the police records in the Village of Etal. "Surely this can't be Guido." He turned to Joseph the systems operator.

"Your eminence I have patched into the crime reports on their computer. The man killed at the Castle Inn, by Lotar Herron, had to be Guido. We have not had contact with him for over eighteen hours, now, and his homing device does not track. Maria Albrecht was in the record as a witness."

"How can this be?" said the Bishop slowly, in a very low voice. "He was too well trained to have this happen."

"Sir, perhaps his appetite just got the better of him."

"What do you mean 'appetite'? said the Bishop angrily.

"If you will pardon my frankness, sir: his sexual appetite. I saw how excited he became when we were viewing Maria Albrecht and Ruth Reilly."

The Bishop shrugged and looked away. "Now I will have to use some one else. Contact his operative in Paris for me immediately!"

With all the power, the money, the elaborate communications network, and the dedicated membership, the Bishop was frustrated at the occasional failures. His organization had bailed the Vatican out of financial difficulties, from ineptness with their world bank. The Pope had even given the Opus Dei special dispensation to work independently from the Vatican hierarchy. He had made inroads into the security system of the United States and other powerful countries. At times, he felt that he had the power of the universe within his grasp, only to see it slip away, because of the incompetence and lack of tenacity of his followers. Where was he going to find people he could trust that didn't allow their carnal desires to make them such fools?

The Bishop knew he must exercise his private communication privilege with the Pope. *I must collect my thoughts, succinctly, so that the Pope in his advanced state of senility may make his decisions without much thought, based upon my recommendations. I must be sure that the Vatican is not infiltrated with spies. There is no choice but for me to go to Rome, immediately. The Carmerlengo must be alerted by me, in person.*

CHAPTER 36

▼

BISHOP RHEIN AND MARIA

Maria could hardly believe her eyes. Bishop Rhein was in his late eighties and physically slight but his mind was sharp and his eyes exhibited humor and compassion. "Maria, my child, it is so wonderful to see you." She hugged him and could feel how frail he had become.

"Dear father, you are like a long lost relative to me." She wiped away her tears. "We thought you had been taken away and I could never see you again."

"How is your mother, Angelina?" he said, with a look of concern.

Lotar was waiting outside watching the farmers go about their daily chores of milking and cleaning out the stalls of the large dairy herd. The barns and the barnyards were well tended, swept, whitewashed, neat and orderly. The Bishop had been hidden in a comfortable apartment over the milking parlor since his disappearance from the Cathedral. The sect of farmers lived in a communal compound, away from the mainstream of the community. This was a natural hiding place since they permitted little contact with the outside world. They watched over the Bishop at the request of Lotar.

"She is fine, but working too hard at the pension."

"Maria I must tell you some things about your background that few persons know. It is important for your safety that you be told. I may not have much time left. The order of the Church where I have spent my life has become tainted with mistrust and suspicion. I have been ridiculed for my beliefs and hunted to quiet my knowledge." His expression grew sad and concerned.

"Father you don't have to tell me anything?"

"Wait child, please be quiet and listen. You do not understand. I must tell you things about both your father and your mother. These things must be kept secret for the good of our people and for future generations. If the church should find out these things it could have a great negative impact allowing the forces of evil ability to do more damage to our civilization. Your life is involved."

Maria was wide eyed with anticipation.

"Your mother is a very special person." He hesitated and looked down at his trembling hands. "Your father is alive and known to her and to me. He holds a very high position in the Catholic Church at the Vatican. He, in fact, is in charge of the Vatican's hidden archives. I have sent him a secret communication but I do not know if he ever received it. He may not know about your birth or that he has you as a daughter. He probably would not believe it. Positive identification can be made through a DNA test if he could be persuaded to submit to it."

Maria was bursting with questions, but waited.

"You and your mother share secrets that neither of you are aware of. Your father was not an ordained priest when you were conceived, but really only a child himself. He went away from our village and the cathedral to receive intensive training at the Vatican. His proficiency in languages, his personality and his general intellect caused him to be one of the hand picked few that go into the order for administrative training without ever working as a priest in a parish."

Maria could wait no longer; "Father, who is this man? When can I see him?"

Bishop Rhein looked at her intently and slumped in his chair for a moment, as if dosing off to sleep. He took a deep breath and said, "We have to find out more about him and his beliefs and then we can possibly arrange that."

"But what about my mother?"

"Are you familiar with the Holy Grail?"

Surprised, she said, "Isn't that some kind of chalice or something used at the "Last Supper?"

The Bishop's voice was becoming very faint; "There are many stories about the Grail and what has become of it. Are you familiar with DaVinci's painting of the "Last Supper?"

"I have seen paintings of the "Last Supper" but I am not sure who the artist was."

"There are many versions," he said, "but DaVinci's is the most prominent and recognized in the Christian Religion. The Holy Grail has been said to exist since the time of Christ. The search for it has continued for two thousand years. Now what you must understand; we don't know for sure if the Grail was an object or objects used by Christ or whether it was a person or a religious concept."

Maria was becoming very confused. "How does this relate to my mother?"

"You must carefully study the painting. The answers are there."

At that moment, Lotar Herron burst into the room. "We have been discovered. There are people here to take Bishop Rhein away. We must leave immediately. There is a back door where we can escape."

Bishop Rhein sat back in his chair, closed his eyes and said, "I will flee no more. Please Maria, go!"

Lotar from previous agreement with the Bishop grabbed Maria and literally dragged her away. They jumped in the car hidden in one of the barns and drove through a pasture to the main highway.

"How could you leave Bishop Rhein there like that? He is defenseless. He was about to tell me about my mother and father. I must go back to him or I will never know."

Lotar's hands gripped the steering wheel tightly while he sped over the narrow, winding road. "Maria, you don't understand. The Bishop demanded that I take you away for your safety. The answers you seek will be revealed to you. I have some of them. Your father is a man named Dominick Averti. He is a high ranking guardian of the Vatican secret archives, but he does not know about you."

"Why has he never been told? I must go see him."

"You can't do that. It could endanger both of you, and, your mother."

"What about my mother? What was Bishop Rhein referring to when he said, "She is a very special person"?"

"I don't know that answer. Only Bishop Rhein knows that."

"Why did that man at the Castle try to kill me? What do you have to do with a Catholic Bishop?"

Lotar thought for a moment, "Maria, I am a member of the Knights Templar sworn to protect the freedoms and the secrets handed down from the beginning of the Christian religion. It would seem that with Bishop Rhein being a high ranking Catholic, we would be directly opposed to each other. But, that is not it at all."

"We, in fact, have the same goals. He became an outsider to the Catholic hierarchy because he was dedicated to protection of the truth. We have compelling evidence that Mary Magdalene was a good woman and as Jesus' survivor, she was supposed to take his place at the head of the church. The opposing forces among the disciples told lies about her in order to steal her power."

"The man that tried to kill you was a member of the Opus Dei, an organization dedicated to the destruction of the lost books and documents of the Bible that are outside the Vatican archives. They have actually been given power by the Pope to do what ever it takes to make sure that these secrets are known only to the Vatican. The power of the entire organization of the Catholic Church is at stake."

"Mr. Herron, I am deeply grateful for everything you have done for me, but I must go to Rome. Nothing can stop me. I must see my father!"

Lotar thought for a while, and in his frustration, said nothing.

CHAPTER 37

▼

CONVERGENCE ON ROME, DAVID, GLORIA PEOLE, NANCY'S ARRIVAL

With all the persons landing in Rome it seemed as if their weight would tip the "Boot" into the Mediterranean Sea. David had already landed and checked into his hotel. Nancy was in route to spend a few days in Paris before meeting David. Maria was driving to Rome accompanied by a protesting Lotar Herron. The Bishop from the Opus Dei was flying in his private jet from New York to Rome. Ruth Reilly had slipped away from her father, Frank, in the Catskills, after the informative visit from David Schilling, and left on a flight from LaGuardia, determined to find her mother.

Monsignor Dominick Averti was oblivious to all the energy pointed his direction. He knew only of a meeting with Nancy Reilly and was looking forward to giving her limited information from the Vatican archives. His only real goal in life was the protection of the energy, the secrets and the power of the church. He had forsaken all worldly pleasures for his beliefs that the church had the best interests of mankind in its grasp. Nothing could stop him from doing his part. His only ambivalence was what he knew about Nancy, that she didn't know.

———

David was shocked at Gloria Peole. She had taken him a tour of the night life in Rome, after agreeing to be his guide for the next several days. Their last stop was at a restaurant away from tourists, with a band playing traditional Italian folk songs. Gloria had looked attractive and professional in her uniform with her hair in a bun. She excused herself and went to the ladies room. While David was waiting, dancers were performing to the music. A crescendo from the band, a spot light at the center of the floor, and a dancer entered with long flowing dark hair in a red dress. She was the most gorgeous creature he had ever seen dancing in circles around the floor to the applause of the patrons. My God! It was Gloria.

The waiter came to his table. "Senor", he said, "You are with the most beautiful woman in all Italy. She was Miss Italy in the Miss World contest last year."

David had had no idea. Gloria was modest and unassuming about her accomplishments and had made no mention of the contest. She finished her dance to thunderous applause and came back to the table smiling.

"Wow, you are full of surprises!" David was virtually speechless after that.

"It is nothing, just dances I learned as a little girl."

The taxi dropped Gloria off at her apartment and David at his hotel. He was really exhausted after the flight and the excitement of the evening. *If only that girl was twenty years older—stop dreaming. Nancy will be here tomorrow evening. I have lots of landmarks to visit tomorrow, before the Vatican visit.* He fell asleep immediately.

The next morning was clear and the entire day was spent touring the artworks in Rome with Gloria. She was very well trained. Thank God he had decided to use a guide, considering the number of sites they visited. It would have taken him two or three days on his own. He had to get back to his hotel in late afternoon to meet Nancy after her arrival at DaVinci airport. He had counted eighty two monuments, sites, and artworks in Rome from the guidebook that were compelling to a serious tourist. With the entire contents of the Vatican yet to be seen, he wondered if the two weeks in Italy would be enough. The Colosseum, the Pantheon, the Fountains, the Tiber river bridges, the churches, the various tombs, the Arches, the Forums, the temples, the theatres; it seemed as if all civilization had passed through and left its mark on this city.

———

Nancy walked through the arrival gate carrying her laptop computer, her purse, and a significant backpack. She looked excited but a little tired. "Hi, David. Thank you for meeting me. It's nice to see you."

"Nancy, how are you? How was the flight?"

"It was exhausting but thank goodness I slept a lot of the way. Have you been waiting here long? How do you like Rome?"

"It is a completely fascinating city. I am totally overwhelmed by the sights. Please let me carry your bags for you."

The taxi driver drove as if he were in a speed trial for a European racing event. Nancy and David were both relieved to get to the hotel without an accident. They had a light dinner and drinks at the hotel restaurant.

While finishing her coffee, Nancy said, "I am looking forward to a good nights sleep to be fresh for our appointment at the Vatican tomorrow. What time are we supposed to be there?"

"Our appointment with Monsignor Averti is not until eleven o'clock. I thought that a later time would give you an opportunity to rest and prepare for the next several days."

"Thank you, David. That is very considerate of you. If you don't mind I am ready to go to my room and crash."

He realized that the presence of this enchanting woman had erased all thoughts of Gloria Peole. "I am tired too. It was an entirely whirl wind day visiting Roman landmarks."

He left her on her floor at the elevator and went to his room to find his message light blinking. It was Ruth Reilly's father, Frank. "Mr. Schilling I found your hotel phone number from Nancy's itinerary. Could you please call me or have Nancy call me when she arrives. Ruth got away from me in the mountains and left a note that she is coming to Rome to find her mother."

Oh dear! Now what should I do? David called Nancy's room but there was no answer. He decided to give her the message in the morning.

Maria and Lotar were entering Northern Italy while the Bishop from Opus Dei was landing at a private airport in Rome. Ruth Reilly's flight would arrive later. Guido's substitute operative for the Opus Dei was already at work.

CHAPTER 38

▼

ROME—THE NEXT DAY

David awakened refreshed to the early morning sun streaming in from his balcony. He spent thirty minutes doing daily aerobic exercises while finishing a pot of coffee. There was still plenty of time for a brisk walk before meeting Nancy at breakfast. He checked the emails on his laptop computer and found nothing but junk mail. Outdoors, in the brisk morning air, he felt as light as a feather in his tennis shoes and warm up suit. The city was just beginning to come alive with service trucks speeding through the streets. He was headed for the park where there was no traffic.

His departure from the hotel was being watched.

At 9:00 Nancy walked through the double doors into the patio restaurant in a light weight khaki blouse and skirt. Her outfit almost matched his. Her smile was radiant and her deep blue eyes sparkling as she approached his table.

"Nancy I have something to tell you," David said while pouring her coffee. She looked up expectantly.

"Your daughter is on her way here to Rome. Her flight will land here late this morning. I had a message from your ex husband, Frank, at my room last night."

"But that can't be. She is in the Catskills with him."

"She slipped away from him and left a note that she was coming here to find you because you are in some kind of danger. When I made the trip to the Catskills to confirm her safety she was extremely stressed and determined to find you because of all the threats."

"You and I both know that the 'danger' is our research. Should we just stop what we are doing and go home? Now what am I going to do about Ruth? We have had this appointment with Monsignor Averti scheduled. What did you want to tell me about him?"

David said, "Let's take one thing at a time. Maybe I can get the guide Gloria Peole to find out when Ruth is arriving and meet her at the airport."

"The airlines won't give anyone passenger information. How can that work?"

"Gloria works for the airlines. I am sure she can find out."

"That would be great if she can meet Ruth. What is the mystery about Dominick Averti?"

David hesitated, "It is just that he may be part of the operative system for the Opus Dei. Since the Pope has given them independence and immunity we have to be very careful to approach Averti cautiously until we find out where he stands."

"He has been friendly and helpful. I can't imagine he is dangerous."

David leaned over the table and said in a very low voice, "We must never under estimate what power can do, even disguised by the church. The good works for its followers may be secondary to the needs of the power structure."

David found Gloria Peole at her cellular phone number. She agreed to find Ruth and bring her to the hotel.

The Bishop from Opus Dei was in a limousine on his way to the Vatican. The Pope was alerted to his arrival and was clearing his calendar for the meeting.

Their relationship was not as friends but one of necessary alliance, the type reserved for heads of state.

CHAPTER 39

▼

THE POPE AND THE BISHOP

The Bishop from Opus Dei was slightly perturbed by the thorough security of the Swiss Guard. He was used to having his way, even with the Pope. The Carmerlengo greeted him and led him through large double doors into the Pope's quarters. The Bishop kneeled and paid proper respects.

"Please rise and be seated my son." The Bishop was shocked at how frail the Pope was compared to their last visit.

"Thank you for receiving me on such short notice your holiness."

In weak and broken English, the Pope said, "You have matters of great importance. What are they?"

"I fear that our archives are in danger of being revealed to an outsider, one that could do great damage to the Church."

"We have the most trusted keeper of the archives. What is the problem?"

"I fear that Dominick Averti's competence may be compromised by issues from his personal life."

"This man has had no personal life. He has been groomed by the Church for his position since he was a child." The Pope was growing agitated by the suggestion of mis-trust.

"Information about his relationships has come to my attention that places the Church in peril. He may be meeting with two persons that seek information from the archives, as we speak."

"You mean they are here, now?"

"Yes, and the meeting must be stopped." The Bishop told him the astounding private information about Dominick.

The Pope turned to the Carmerlengo. "Bring me the commander of the Swiss Guard and his chief of security, immediately."

CHAPTER 40

▼

IN THE ARCHIVES

Nancy and David had already passed through level one and level two of the Vatican archives and were waiting for positive identification from the palm prints that were scanned through the security machine. Level three was accessible to only a few persons in the world. Dominick was to meet them there.

Maria and Lotar arrived at the entrance gate by taxi. The Swiss Guard, at the gate, would not acknowledge that Dominick Averti was here or he was in charge of the archives. Lotar was prepared for the difficulty and pressed the button of a transmitter in his pocket. Members of the Knights Templar were waiting nearby to execute the emergency plan.

———

Gloria was waiting at the Leonardo DaVinci airport for Ruth's arrival. She was smiling but pre-occupied with the tasks in front of her.

———

Finally they were cleared into level three. Nancy and David stepped into an open space and the door was closed and sealed behind them. Descending in the small elevator was like the closed in feeling of a mausoleum.

The doors opened to a brightly lighted and musty smelling room. Dominick was waiting. He was grey around the temples but still movie star handsome. As he approached them, smiling, Nancy once again experienced her strange sensation when Dominick was near.

"Nancy, you look wonderful." He grasped her hand in both of his. Turning to David he said, "You must be David Schilling; welcome."

"We are very excited and grateful for the opportunity to be in the Vatican archives," David said. Nancy was speechless.

There were doors leading to passage ways at the outside of the room. David wondered if these led to the crypts, and secret tunnels, from the ancient city and the foundations of buildings that had once occupied this site. He imagined that he could feel the history of civilization radiating upward into this room. The things he knew about the Monsignor from Bishop Rhein gave him a sense of caution. *How can I get the information we need and get Nancy and myself out of here safely?*

Nancy said, "Monsignor, you have been so generous to allow us this visit. I know that there are archivists throughout the world that would do anything to have this opportunity." Dominick smiled. Nancy said, "I have received word that my daughter, Ruth, is on her way here from New York and is being picked up at the airport. Is there any possibility that she could accompany us in this research?"

"That would be highly irregular. I would have to check with my superiors."

Sirens were blaring at the front gate where Knights Templar operatives had made an attempt to enter a restricted area. The security force of the Swiss Guard was rushing there to apprehend them.

In the confusion, Lotar grabbed Maria by the arm and pushed her inside a door leading to a stairway. They were inside the Vatican restricted area, and had now only to find the way to get to level three. Lotar's knowledge of the Vatican layout was from Templar intelligence.

———

The flight landed on time. Gloria saw Ruth walking out of the entrance ramp and immediately recognized her from the identification photos. "Hello, Ruth Reilly?"

"Yes, I am Ruth Reilly. Who are you?"

"My name is Gloria Peole. I was asked to meet you by your mother and David Schilling."

"Oh, where are they?"

"They are in a meeting at the Vatican right now. That is why they asked me to help you get to the hotel."

"Well thank you but I must get to the Vatican to see my mother first."

"I believe they are spending time in the secret archives. You and I can not go in there."

"What do you have to do with my mother and with David Schilling?"

"I met David Schilling on his flight from Rome and have been his tour guide for the past two days. They could not arrange another appointment in the archives so your mother asked me to meet you."

"Look I don't know you but I have to trust you. I have reason to believe that my mother's life is in danger. I must get to her immediately."

Gloria stepped back and just looked at her. "I have explored all the area around the Vatican as a child. If it is that urgent, I may be able to get us into secret entrances not known to others. Are you willing to take chances?"

"Of course," "I must see her."

They had the taxi drop Ruth's bags at the hotel and then take them to a place with narrow streets and old buildings. There was a small cemetery area and an entrance to an alley. Gloria led her to a dead end in the alley. She stood for a moment then stomped her foot a number of times on the pavement. A very narrow door concealed in the brick wall opened. They entered and began descending a winding stairway lighted only by the flashlight from Gloria's purse. When they arrived at a tunnel far below the surface they could hear creatures scurrying around in the darkness. Ruth had cold chills from her fear of darkness and creatures of the night.

"I don't know why you are doing this for me and I don't know what I can do if we find her. I just have to warn her of the danger."

Gloria said, "I was very impressed with David Schilling and his research mission. I am studying some of his interests at the university and want to help in any way I can." It was growing colder as they descended and the air was stale making breathing difficult.

CHAPTER 41

▼

THE CONFLICT

The head of security of the Swiss Guard entered and bowed to the Pope. "You must go to Monsignor Averti in the Archives and tell him to stop the tour with his visitors."

"But your holiness, we have no access to the third level. We only secure the entrances. Our surveillance system watches and listens to persons in the archives at all times. What do you fear is at risk so that we may take action?"

The Pope gathered his energy and said, "The Ark of the Covenant, the Holy Grail, the lost books of the Bible, the Dead Sea Scrolls, the Rosetta Stone; have you heard of these things?"

The Bishop and the head of security looked at each other. "Do you mean these things are there and at risk?" asked the guard.

"The entire security of the Catholic Church and the secrets of the formation of the Christian religion are at risk. You must put me in touch with Averti immediately!" The Pope was energized with his anxiety.

Dominick had left the third level with David and Nancy and was descending outside the range of the security surveillance system. He had to find out what they knew and exactly what was their mission and then decide what must be done to protect the works of the Church. He had to show them things that were off limits and engage them in conversation to get the information he needed.

Nancy was innocently oblivious and as excited as a child at Christmas, while David had shattering information from Bishop Rhein that he could not reveal. They stood in front of a small room that looked like a jail cell with sealed entrance doors. The lighting was subdued as they entered the first door and waited for it to close behind them. Then the entrance door to the room opened to an area not larger than fifteen feet square.

Dominick engaged a climate control apparatus, waited for a moment, and then opened a sealed closet. He carried its contents to a table and carefully laid the objects down. There were documents, books, and metal and stone artifacts.

———

The communications device sounded harmlessly at level three with the Pope waiting to speak to Monsignor Averti. "Your holiness there is no response," said the Swiss security officer.

"We must contact him immediately. What is wrong?" The Pope was highly irritated.

"Your holiness the only thing I can think of is that they descended below level three where there is no coverage by our surveillance system."

"But that is impossible," said the Pope. "No one is permitted to enter the levels below without another authorized archivist."

———

"What do you wish to accomplish with your research?' said Dominick while standing between David and Nancy, and the table, with the objects.

Nancy and David looked at each other as if waiting for the formation of an answer and permission to speak. Finally, David said, "We have only one goal in mind. The confusion and the contradictions of history, the forgeries, the wars, the suppression and destruction of information, raises questions about the validity of the Bible, Jesus Christ, Mary Magdalene, and the true authors and protectors of civilization. We hope only to apply rational answers from the references, adapt them to the modern society, and to explain these theories to the world."

Dominick's worst fears were being realized. "How could you hope to help mankind with this kind of effort?"

Nancy said, "Monsignor, we believe that there is a common thread of continuity of civilization starting in Sumeria thousands of years before Christ. The Moslems, the Jews, the Christians and most other forms of the recognition of God, all stem from the same roots. Greed and power has divided the people and pitted them against one another. We hope for some small part in a movement back to the common ground of the beginning."

"No one knows the truth about the beginning. We must have faith in our teachings."

David said, "Yes that is true, but if we find the lies and the forgeries along with the true documentation whether it be in lost books, buildings, buried civilizations or whatever, can't we peel away the outer layer of wrongs as you would peel a banana, so we can get to the heart or the fruit of truth?"

"You are saying that for thousands of years we have been killing each other out of ignorance while we actually are all brothers from the same place? Don't you admit that there is only one true God of the universe?"

"Of course," said David. The difference in God is only our perception. God has not changed. Only our respective viewpoints of God change."

While Monsignor Dominick Averti was somewhat of a free thinker, the indoctrination from the Church starting with his early childhood could not let his mind open to all the possibilities. This would be like some of the soul searching dormitory discussions at late night by his seminary class mates. He usually walked out of these discussions knowing there was no answer—no solution. He was growing more and more uncomfortable with the idea that these two people could walk out of here and create havoc in the church and the world. Even his relationship with Nancy could not override this issue.

———

The Bishop from Opus Dei, from his success with extremist measures, was busy convincing the Pope that Nancy and David were dangerous and must never be allowed to leave the Vatican. He had an operative already at work inside the Vatican so that they could act with or without the blessing of the Pope. *I must excuse myself from the Pope and contact my operative.* He had the communications device in his pocket.

———

With inside help Lotar and Maria were making steady progress towards level three. "Mr. Herron how is it that you have contacts, here, inside the Vatican? Isn't this supposed to be one of the most secure places in the world?"

"Maria, absolute security is a myth. There are always persons inside any organization that can and will reveal secret information. Even the American intelligence system, with their FBI and CIA, has been infiltrated by the Opus Dei. It is reasonable that there would be Knights Templar informants, here, inside the Vatican."

"How much danger are we in? Before you answer, I don't care. I must find the man that is supposed to be my Father. Please, let's hurry!"

———

Gloria and Ruth were actually weaving their way through a series of tunnels far below the surface of the earth. The custom of building new structures, neighborhoods, cities on top of old ones was evident from the things they saw with Gloria's flashlight. *I hope to God these batteries don't give out or we will be lost underground forever,* thought Gloria.

They were hand in hand to avoid stumbling over rocks or crashing into overhead obstacles. Gloria stopped and turned back to Ruth. "We seem to have come to a dead end. I was sure that this passage way would lead us to an opening in the archives. I must stop and think. I was only a little girl when I was last here."

CHAPTER 42

▼

THE MEETING

David carefully turned the pages of a priceless original document after putting on the surgical gloves furnished by Dominick. "This is a strange feeling, like being transported back in history, and intruding into a land and a time where we don't belong."

"These preserved documents are from various periods over the past thousands of years and are composed of many different substances, each of which reacts differently. For example, David, the page you are handling will disintegrate if exposed to the oil of your fingers and the nitrogen rich normal air." Dominick was speaking softly but was poised to intervene at David's slightest mistake.

Nancy, deep in concentration, was examining a stone tablet and making notes. Dominick was watching her from the corner of his eye.

After an hour in the small vault Dominick said, "We must leave this room and go to the large outer chamber where we can talk. The composition of the air in here can become toxic after too much exposure."

They went back through the sealed doors. Dominick led them to another large room with a high domed ceiling. He turned the on lights to expose a breathtaking sight. The stars, the sun, the moon, the oceans, the mountains were all depicted in a panoramic scene above, around them and below their feet. In one area of the circular room was a reproduction of DaVinci's painting, The Last Supper. The huge cavern had been developed from ages past, to now, with depictions from the crucifixion to a chart showing the migration of civilizations about the earth. There were historical scenes including the crusades, the Romans, the Celtics, the Knights Templars, the pyramids, and other biblical events. The room was used to indoctrinate only the highest and most trusted members of the Catholic hierarchy.

They were sitting on a stone bench in the center of the room mesmerized by the scene around them. David recognized the Masonic symbols of the square and compass. Nancy rose and turned slowly to view the scenes. "May I take pictures here with my digital camera, Monsignor?"

"No I am sorry Nancy, pictures are forbidden. Even entry to this room is forbidden. I should not have brought you here. This is a place for training of a privileged few in the Church."

"Why did you allow us to come in here, Dominick?" said Nancy.

Dominick's head was bowed and he slowly looked up at Nancy with a piercing gaze into her eyes. "You don't remember me do you?"

Perplexed, she said, "What do you mean 'remember you', I have known you for several years"

"You have known me even longer than for several years, Nancy."

A noise caused them to look at the doorway to see Ruth and Gloria standing there. They were all speechless for a moment, and then Dominick rushed to them. "Who are you? How did you get in here?"

Dominick grabbed Ruth and while they were standing side by side Nancy screamed, "Oh my God!" The resemblance between Dominick and Ruth was like a mirror image. "Now I remember," Nancy said, as she clasped her hands to the side of her head.

But this can't be. Dominick is the father of Ruth, the man I met in Rome many years ago while I was a flight attendant. Then there was no miracle with Frank fathering Ruth. His sperm analysis was negative when we failed in an attempt to have another child after Ruth. I married him only two weeks after my experience with Dominick in Rome. Not knowing I was pregnant.

Ruth and Dominick stared at each other, stunned. The light of recognition was in both their faces. Dominick knew immediately.

"Mother are you all right?' said Ruth while looking past Dominick.

"Yes, darling but I have things to tell you."

At that point, two other intruders appeared at the doorway. Lotar and Maria had made their way through the secret passageways to find them.

Dominick was completely shocked at the presence of all these people in an area that had been protected and off limits over the ages. Now, under his supervision, the security of the church was at risk.

David stepped forward. "Maria, Lotar, how did you get in here? What are you doing here?"

Gloria was receiving a message in the hidden ear piece she was wearing. She looked away from the group to concentrate.

Maria just stared at Dominick not speaking. David looked at Maria, and then at the Da Vinci painting and back again.

Dominick went to Lotar, who was towering over him and said, "Who are you? How did you get in here?"

Lotar said quietly, "I have brought someone here that had to meet you, your daughter."

Now everyone was speechless and staring at Lotar, Maria and Dominick.

▼

THE REVELATIONS

With everyone talking at once, David stepped up to moderate the confusion. In the meantime the Pope had become ill and had to be put to bed. His doctor was summoned. The Bishop from Opus Dei was contacting his operative inside the archives.

Outside, a beautiful day greeted tourists to the Vatican. St. Peter's Basilica towered over the paved area casting shadows in relief from the sun. Visitors from all over the globe in their Nike shoes, shorts, and jump suits were happily taking pictures and enjoying the festive atmosphere of this historic site. Everyone was oblivious to the drama taking place inside the Vatican.

Dominick's emotions overpowered his need to speak. The inside of his head seemed to swell with alarms ringing and explosions taking place. *Could this beautiful red head, green eyed woman be the daughter that Bishop Rhein wrote about to him in his code letter?*

Maria was equally mesmerized, frozen in place as she stared at Dominick.

Holy mother of God! Must I summon the Guards? I have allowed a security breach that will destroy me and the church. The emotions in the room were like the crescendo of a fireworks display. Everyone had questions. No one had all the answers.

David turned his back on Lotar and Maria, walked to the center of the cavern and said, "Please calm down and listen to me. It is obvious that there is great cause for alarm here, but we must sort out the facts."

"Lotar Herron, you introduced Maria, here, as Monsignor Averti's daughter. I can verify that from my meeting with Bishop Rhein in the alpine Village before he disappeared. That is startling but there is another secret about her that only Bishop Rhein and I know. Also there is a remarkable resemblance between Dominick Averti and Ruth Reilly."

Nancy looked up at the frescoed ceiling in anguish and said, "My darling Ruth for all these years I did not know but now I know that your real father is Dominick Averti."

Everyone started talking at once. "Mother, how can that be? What about my father Frank?"

Nancy said, "He can not be your real father. We tried for years to have another child after you but Frank tested sterile. We thought that your conception and birth was a miracle. You must know that I was here, in Rome, just two weeks before my marriage to Frank. I met Dominick one night in a café. That was when it happened. For all these years I did not know until I saw the two of you side by side."

Ruth and Maria both went to Dominick, one on each side, and grasped his arms. Dominick had tears flowing down his cheeks.

Ruth looked at Maria and said, "But this means you are my sister."

"Yes," gasped Maria. "I had no idea." They took each others hands.

Lotar was standing quietly in the background. David again stepped forward, "There is something else we must be aware of, here, that could change the course of history."

Everyone turned to look at David. "Maria was attacked in the castle at Etal by a member of the Opus Dei that tried to kill her to keep her identity from being known. Lotar, here, saved her life."

Maria said, "Why would they want to kill me to keep my father's identity a secret?"

"Maria, would you please come with me and stand in front of the copy of the painting of "The Last Supper."

He positioned her so that she was side by side with the life size figure of Mary Magdalene, sitting at the right hand of Jesus.

Everyone in the room was silent while looking at the painting and then at Maria. She and Mary Magdalene were identical.

"We must take this secret to our graves. You are the descendent of Mary Magdalene and Jesus Christ, the only one in the world other than your Mother, Angelina."

While watching and listening to all this, Gloria was receiving a message from the Bishop of the Opus Dei, "You must not let anyone leave the archives alive. It is time for you to do what you were trained to do."

Gloria took a canister from her purse, went to the center of the room, climbed up on the bench, and held the object high above her head. "Dominick Averti, we must protect the church. I have poison gas in this canister. None of you move. If I drop this canister we will all die within seconds."

"But who are you?" Dominick was in shock.

"I have received my orders directly from the Pope through the Bishop of the Opus Dei." Gloria said in a determined voice. Her dark hair and her dark eyes accented by the drama made her even more beautiful than before.

"You must wait," said David. There are many questions here, but no one needs to die."

Maria weighed down by all the information about Dominick, her father, and the deity of her mother and her, said, "Yes there are questions. How can Mary Magdalene or my Mother and I with red hair, fair skin and green eyes be related? How could she have been with Jesus in a land of people with dark skin and dark eyes? Aren't we of Celtic descent from Ireland or Scotland?"

David said, "The Celtics or Kelts as they were known in the period from 600 to 400 B.C. were actually from Northern Italy in the Alps. They were barbarians, fair skinned, blond and sometimes with red hair. They challenged the Romans and actually helped bring down the Roman Empire. They spread throughout Europe, Asia and Northern Africa until they finally migrated to Ireland and Scotland. They left no written history, but instead passed their customs by word of mouth. There is theory, that of the six billion people on this planet, one billon are of Celtic descent."

Nancy said, "So you believe that Mary Magdalene was a Celtic in the Holy land and became Jesus' consort?"   .

David said, "This and the fact that the family of Angelina and Maria have been tracked through the centuries, to now, with their direct link to Jesus."

Lotar Herron finally spoke up and said, "I can verify that from my sources with the Knights Templar."

Dominick now knew that his life was over. In this room were his offspring from the only two times in his life to have sexual union. He had spent all his years in the loneliness of the church with only his contact with God for company. He knew he had to act for the benefit of the church, to maintain its power and the good deeds it could do. *If a few have to die to save millions, so be it. If Maria's identity is revealed and should she be regarded as the second coming of Christ, all of civilization could be at risk with religious wars.*

Dominick walked to the bench and climbed up to stand beside Maria. "My friends, and my dear children, I have lived all my life inside the church with vows of poverty and celibacy. Now, at this stage of my life, the irony is that from my sins, two beautiful daughters have come to me. All of you are innocent but many times in history the innocent have had to die in the fight for the eternal lives of men. You will all rest in heaven while I will burn in eternal Hell for my sins."

With tears streaming down her face, Nancy shouted, "But Dominick we can survive this. You have done great works. Please allow your self to be mortal and forgive yourself as God has taught us to forgive."

"Nancy, you don't understand the foundation of what I have been sworn to protect. I have no choice."

Ruth and Maria, newly found sisters, arm in arm were comforting each other.

"Gloria, give me the canister," said Dominick in a determined voice. "May God forgive all of you for your sins and that I will be made to pay for what I must do." He raised the canister over his head to throw it to the floor.

"But Monsignor Averti," shouted David, "The revelations of Jesus could allow millions of people to have direct contact with God, and to be saved for eternity.

"No, you don't understand," said Dominick, his face distorted in agony. The Church must assemble our people so we can place them in contact with God. What is happening here could destroy all the structure. We must speak for them."

"But the Bible doesn't demand a large congregation or an agent for me or any-one to speak directly with God!" David was walking closer to Dominick and Gloria on the bench.

"Stay back. I can't let you leave this room. This young woman and I must complete our task and pray to God that the others here will be forgiven. This canister must be smashed for the good of man."

"Oh Lord, my God, is there no help for the widow's son?" shouted Lotar Herron. Only he, David and Nancy knew the meaning of this plea.

A small area in the floor opened and the bench with Gloria and Dominick fell into the darkness. Then the floor closed.

David, Nancy, Ruth, Maria, and Lotar stood there in shock. The lights in the huge grotto shone brightly. Maria and Ruth were sobbing. David started to probe about the room looking for an access to the trap door that had taken Dominick and Gloria. Nancy stood, speechless, trying to understand what had happened, fearful of what was next. Then a general confused conversation began.

At the height of hysteria, Lotar, in his rich baritone voice, bellowed, "You must be quiet and listen to me.

All stopped and turned to Lotar. He was a strong, powerful, and majestic presence. His training and time on the stage served him well. There was no one else in the room with his grasp of the situation.

With center stage and with everyone's attention, he said, "Our first response, here, is survival."

A burst of questions arose.

He held up his hands for attention. "My friends, we must stay calm. There are many things in this place we can not understand.

A quiet expectation was on all faces.

"We can do nothing about Monsignor Averti and Gloria. They may re-appear and they may not. We can not go to the Vatican officials."

David interrupted, "Surely Mr. Herron, we must report this happening to someone. What about the authorities?"

"You must remember, the Vatican is a sovereign country and not ruled by Roman or Italian governments. Any act other than our escape could place us all in jeopardy." The delivery of Lotar's words to David was stern.

"Of course you are right," said David. "Do you have any idea what has happened?"

Lotar walked to the wall, where there was a cut away view of one the Pyramids at Giza. The genius of the architects' protective devices, built into this structure, was carefully detailed. He pointed to the tombs. "Pharaohs entombed, there, were protected from grave robbers for centuries. The robbers and many legitimate archeologists have been trapped, and carried away in the devices, never to be seen again."

Now he had everyone's full attention. "The technology was designed under this grotto, where we stand, hundreds, maybe thousands of years ago, and forgotten as the disaster and the plunder of each new conqueror took place.

Earthquakes, volcanic eruptions and the debris from the destruction and the rebuilding of countless temples, arenas, and structures of government, were piled, layer upon layer over ruins of past civilizations, until they were forgotten.

"Adding to this phenomenon was each ruler's disdain and deliberate destruction of documents and the historic artifacts of his predecessor."

David spoke up, "Surely some documents survived all this. Shouldn't we continue our search for the lost books?"

Lotar, with the look of a patient professor, said, "Any surviving documents during the Dark Ages were buried in urns and stashed in rural areas, catacombs, or under the foundations of buildings. Possession, then and now, could mean death with no questions asked. The surviving material had to be translated and authenticated. Much was lost in this process."

David again interjected, "Some of these grottos were sealed or buried, intact, lost and forgotten. With these traps, designed for death to intruders, and emptying into tunnels, underground rivers, cells, bottomless pits, catacombs—isn't it possible that Dominick and Gloria could survive and that they were not swallowed by these devices for their death?"

Nancy was thinking back over time, *How can we leave here without an effort to save Gloria, and Dominick, the father of my daughter? Ruth is the most precious person in my life. Her safety must come first.*

"Mr. Herron, are you sure that our escape is the only alternative?" Even as she asked this, with all her experiences, Nancy already knew the answer.

Without giving Lotar a chance to answer, David said, "How can we leave here? It looks as if all the entrances are sealed."

Lotar said, "I want all of you to follow me quickly. We can leave the same way Maria and I arrived."

David said, "But if we escape won't we be detained? What right do we have to leave all this mess behind us? Won't we be pursued later?"

"Think about it," Lotar said, impatiently, "The Vatican can not afford to report this and they have no jurisdiction outside here. We must be quiet and try to cut our selves loose from the forces that have been threatening us."

A loud crash into one of the closed entrance doors caused everyone to stand, frozen, then another louder one.

Lotar shouted, "They are after us. Follow me quickly!"

He went to the stone object, square and compass, pressed his hand against the compass hinge, and a door sprung open. He entered the dark tunnel guided by the flashlight he earlier used. As the banging and crashing into another door continued, everyone filed into the tunnel with him. The tunnel door slammed shut leaving the opening undetectable in the lighted room.

Just then the Swiss Guards and the Bishop from Opus Dei burst into the grotto to find it empty. The Bishop tried in vain to reach the Pope's office but there was no signal this far underground.

Meanwhile, Lotar and his entourage made steady progress up the winding stairs, nearing the street level. He stopped just before a wide point where there was a door opening. "We all have places to which we must return. We must go about our jobs and our daily lives while our forces attempt to stop the evil pursuit."

Nancy said, "Mr. Herron, what do we do about the secrets and what we have learned about the possible deity of Maria and her mother, Angelina?"

David spoke up, "We must swear a blood oath upon the heads of Christ and our children, to take these secrets to our graves."

Lotar said, "If everyone agrees to this, please hold hands and I will administer the oath."

With that everyone joined hands. Lotar began, "Lord God please bind us together in silence and with trust so that we each may carry your ministry for the good of all mankind. We hereby swear our secrecy, bound by the pain of death. Amen."

All joined in the saying of, "Amen," then released hands.

Lotar gave final instructions, "When we open this door we will enter inconspicuously into a crowd of tourists. We will then each go our separate ways. May God go with you."

The door opened slowly allowing the sunlight to burst in. The pillars immediately in front kept the group from being blinded and allowed them cover to blend into the crowd of tourists without detection. The area near the Vatican crafts and arts center is constantly immersed with people coming and going in all directions. Of course no one was aware of the life and death drama that had taken place below. The divergent forces that have changed the course of history were still at work and possibly would be for another thousand years.

They walked out into the sunlight to freedom. Nancy, Ruth and Maria were arm in arm.

Nancy, with tears, looked at David and said, "I feel that I have just begun to know you."

David said, "I can only hope that we may continue from here."

The Vatican newspaper reported that Dominick Averti had been mysteriously lost in the underground caverns beneath the Vatican. In the bright sun shiny day the tourists continued their search for amusement. The secrets were safe.

THE END

978-0-595-36767-2
0-595-36767-4

Printed in the United States
39268LVS00007B/51